War

War

Evolution

Rommell C. Lewis

Authored and Published by Rommell C. Lewis, 2016

ISBN-13: 9780692647097
ISBN-10: 0692647090

Author's Note

THIS BOOK IS intended for the mature adult audience. This book is not intended for children, teens, young adults, or anyone who cannot separate fantasy from reality. This book contains offensive scenes and violence, including *sex, murder, killing, swearing, abuse, rape, racism, torture, misogyny, sadomasochism, and religious blasphemy*. If you are an adult who is offended by such material, you are highly advised not to purchase or read this book. This book is a work of fiction, and any relation to any real person, living, dead, or otherwise; locales; and real situations is purely coincidental. Keep this book out of the reach of young children and minors. The author will not be held responsible for any injury, theft, loss of property, damage, or death that resulted from you or anyone else reading this book. This book is for entertainment purposes only.

This book is dedicated to my pet snake, Francis.

The Hunter

Pyongyang, North Korea, August 14, 2165

CORPORAL TIFFANY RAVEN had hoped to spend her three-year deployment tending to the wounded in the base hospital—patching up a few soldiers to send them right back into the fight. Instead she'd received orders to the Seventy-Third Joint Task Force Marines Infantry Battalion as a combat medic.

She'd seen more in three years than most adults could fathom. Bomb-strapped mothers holding their children, entire families slaughtered just for speaking ill of Emperor Jim Puk Tu III. It was time to go home.

Tonight was the last mission—a simple extraction mission. North Koreans had captured Sergeant Major Walker and his squad behind enemy lines as they conducted reconnaissance for a potential ambush site. Intel had located him in a school in central Pyongyang.

The capital had become a shell of its former self. The marines had forced Jim Puk Tu into hiding, and he'd abandoned the capital and left its citizens to fend for themselves, leaving thousands of North Koreans displaced amid the ruins of a crumbling dystopia.

"How ya holding up?" asked Captain Mallory.

She didn't know how to respond to the captain's question. Lie and tell him what he wanted to hear? Or tell him the truth: that she was sick and tired of being sick and tired? Eating the same MREs, sleeping with one eye open or not sleeping at all, watching good men and women die…She had almost forgotten why she'd joined until she had seen the thankful faces of malnourished Koreans enjoying a hot meal in the mess hall.

"Hoorah, sir!"

"Hoorah!" the other soldiers echoed her response.

"That's what I like to hear!" said Captain Mallory. "You guys want the good news or the bad news?"

"There is no good news!"

"Damn straight! This is it, guys! Tomorrow we go home! So make every bullet count! Give these squint-eyed bastards everything you got. Because there is…"

"No tomorrow!"

"Hoorah!"

Despite the explosions and the gunfire pelting off the Humvee, Mallory always kept a smile on his face. Deep down she knew he was scared, just as the rest of his soldiers were, but he couldn't show it. He was their leader, and they were counting on him to make it home alive. His battalion mostly consisted of young men and women—some as young as Raven. Mallory was old enough to be their father. If they completed a three-year tour, they would receive a free ride through college. Mallory had promised each one of them he would be at their graduation.

"Private Leroy!"

"Yes, sir!"

"ETA!"

Private Leroy brought up the Humvee's holographic GPS and sent it to Captain Mallory's head visor.

"Five mike. All right, men! What did I tell you about sticking to SOPs?"

"To hell with SOPs!"

"Hoorah! There ain't nothing standard about war! You get your asses in there! Grab our comrades, and kill anyone who stands in your way!"

"Hoorah!"

The vehicle stopped one hundred yards before the school, allowing them to use the urban terrain as cover.

"Private Leroy! You've got point! Let's move!"

Fifteen years ago, her squad never would have made it this far into Pyongyang. Now only an outpost and crippled vehicles protected what remained. Emperor Jim Puk Tu would fight to the last man.

Fighter jets ripped through the sound barrier above, sprinkling an arsenal of armor-shredding bombs on their targets. MechSoldiers trampled the war zone, obliterating fleeing enemies. Raven gave a thumbs-up to a soldier operating one of the machines, thanking him for clearing a path. She shot a Korean attempting to take out the MechSoldier using a rocket-propelled grenade.

"Hell yeah, Corporal!"

"Show 'em whose boss!"

Raven moved faster, scoring accurate kills. She felt stronger. Unstoppable. Her boots crunched the bones and charred flesh of dead enemy soldiers. She'd become a warrior.

The tide had turned. The joint task force was playing cleanup. Millions of Koreans were freed from the chains of a ruthless tyrant. The streets were stained with the blood of those who had given their lives in the uprising. Their sacrifices would be remembered forever.

Raven watched a bus pull up in front of the school.

"They're trying to move the prisoners! Hustle up!" ordered Mallory. "Command, I need fire support! Get a Mech on that bus!"

That's a negative, Bravo One. Proceed to location and extract the package.

"God damn it!"

The driver fired a heavy laser gun at the squad, pinning them down behind a building.

Sergeant Phelps tossed an antigravity grenade and watched it suck in the driver before spitting him out of a vortex, piece by bloody piece.

The unit got in line formation, and Mallory kicked in the door.

The squad filed in and quickly dispatched two Korean guards, splattering their brains with gunfire—tactics executed with pinpoint precision.

Raven shone her weapon-mounted flashlight down the dark hall. Sweat dripped from her helmet, and the visor's digital readings were clouded from the humidity. Two Koreans guarding a school full of POWs was uncommon. She felt something wasn't right. Their weapons scanned each classroom they passed. Raven remained on their six, periodically checking for enemies. She should have heard cries, screams, or something to tell them what was going on. She heard short bursts of gunfire and an explosion here or there in the distance, but otherwise all was quiet. Too quiet.

Raven listened to the glass crack under her boots, step by step. The school reflected the streets outside—furniture in pieces, blood everywhere, bodies here and there.

They reached a locked double door and took up both sides. Blood trickled from underneath, and they could smell the horrid stench of decomposing flesh. They banged on the door. The soldiers mentally prepared themselves for what horrors awaited them on the other side. Raven saw the sweat and slight shaking of Sergeant Phelps's hands. The young girl, the bravest of them all, could not settle herself.

With one mighty kick, Mallory pushed the door back, revealing its hidden atrocities: bodies, several of them, hanging upside down from the ceiling on meat hooks, their intestines littering the floor, flies and maggots feasting on the remains. The Koreans showed no discrimination. Victims ranged from infant to elderly, all meeting the same fate.

The soldiers spoke not a word to one another, standing in horror at the merciless barbarism of corpses displayed from the ceiling like human chandeliers. Private Leroy's lunch added to the stench. Phelps patted his back until the last of it emptied.

"We still...we still have another floor to clear. Let's keep moving," said Captain Mallory.

Raven saw that the hardened veteran was at a loss for words. But they had to continue. The unit had come this far, and there was no turning back.

Raven shone her light over a staircase leading down into the school cafeteria. A Korean schoolgirl, dressed in a black-and-red-checkered skirt, lay dead on the steps, shot in the head execution style. Raven stepped over the body and kept her weapon trained on the darkness below. She felt soaked and barely able to keep her weapon at eye level. The foyer baked like an oven on a midsummer's day.

"Keep focus." Sensing the slightest weakness in his squad, Captain Mallory was always quick to fix it.

Mallory kept Raven on her toes. She was more than a combat medic, and she wasn't some kid fishing for a free handout. He had requested that Raven stay in the battalion for another three years and then apply for the JTF Academy. She had it in her, and he had always known it.

But Raven hated being forced to do anything she didn't want to do. Life wasn't easy for a kid with no family, raised on the streets of Emerald Colony, eating out of trash cans and stealing clothes to keep warm. Raven made her own decisions.

Still, she feared she would return home after the war and fall back into her old ways or get in with the wrong crowd—all her money liquidized in a needle. Survive three years in Korea but die in one week in Emerald Colony. She'd lost count of how many trust-fund punks, seeking a thrill, shit their pants at the first sight of a roadside bomb, crying for their mommies. Most of them didn't make it past the first week. The liberation of North Korea was no playground.

"Roger, sir," she acknowledged.

A tall soldier in tattered fatigues emerged from behind an overturned desk. "Captain, you gotta get me outta here. She's hot."

"Calm down, Sergeant Major. We're going to get ya out of here. Where are the other troops? Who...who's hot? What are you talking about?"

Mallory used his visor to scan the sergeant major's face for verification. He uploaded the scan and sent it to command.

That's our boy. Good work, team. Send up the others and bring 'em in. We got a hovercraft en route for extraction.

"The child. She's strapped. We gotta go."

Sergeant Major? Raven thought not. He was acting like a spoiled child with only his self-interest in mind.

"Where are the other soldiers, Walker?" asked Mallory.

The man's eyes poured like a leaky faucet. "There are no other soldiers. They're dead."

"What! You forged intel to command just to save your own ass? There are men with families out there dying because of you!"

The troops could not help but look away.

"Where is she?" yelled Mallory.

"We...we...we gotta go."

Mallory spotted the young girl tied to the refrigerator and said, "I'm not leaving her, but I won't think twice of leaving your ass here."

Walker grabbed Leroy's pistol from his drop holster and pointed it Mallory.

"Stand down!" ordered Raven.

She and her team kept Walker in their sights.

"So you're gonna shoot me? Is that it? Then fucking do it!" said Mallory, standing with his arms open.

Thoughts of a court-martial kept Raven's finger on the trigger guard. Shooting a superior NCO would land her a trip to the incinerator.

"You don't know what you're doing," said Walker.

Walker tripped, stepping backward, and fell on his ass. He got up, ran up the stairs to the hovercraft, and left the team with the bomb.

Mallory carefully disconnected each wire from the little girl's vest. Tears streamed down her face as she said something in Korean.

"What's she saying?" asked Raven.

"Mom. She wants her mom."

Her parents were long dead, murdered in cold blood. They had been suspected of using their home to harbor enemy troops. War crimes often went unpunished. As long as it was in the JTF's favor, commanders turned a blind eye.

"Got it! Let's move!"

Raven could almost see Emerald Colony's tall buildings, amid the beautiful Appalachians, resting on the lake's horizon. The sounds, sights, and smells were just out of reach—so close to home, she could taste it. The mission was over. They'd made it.

The poor girl probably would be sent to some orphanage for displaced children and would never learn the truth about her parents. More than likely, she would be told a lie—that they saved her from Korean soldiers—a lie she would carry with her for the rest of her life.

"What's your name, honey?" asked Raven. She looked at Captain Mallory to translate. The hovercraft's cool air blew away the girl's tears, and she spoke in Korean with a smile on her face.

"Kim. Her name is Kim."

"I'm Raven. This is Leroy. Phelps. Mallory."

The little girl smiled at Raven and said, "Wai...wai...n."

"Yeah!" The squad congratulated Kim for learning what probably was her first word in English.

Mallory never took his eyes off Walker. He was silent, his chest heaving beneath his camouflaged armor, his bald head glistening and steaming in the cold.

An all-too-familiar whistle caught Raven's attention. She turned to see a rocket-propelled grenade shot at the hovercraft.

Boom!

She held on tight to Kim, covering her ears. Warning signals blared from the craft's emergency system, and her squad members fell from the sky. Her senses dulled. This was it. The squad's motto, There is no tomorrow, had taken form. If there was a God, he was nowhere to be found. Raven's friends, with whom she had dined, slept, fought, and killed, would perish with her. Would her sacrifices be honored, or would her name end up on some casualty list in a newspaper crumpled and thrown in the trash? Only time would tell.

———

"One more."

"Tiffany, I think you've had enough. Get on home."

"Don't tell me when I've had enough. I said one more!"

The wooden bar was all she could see, yet she sensed his presence getting closer. As he leaned in, the bartender's breath smelled of a tuna sandwich. He whispered into Raven's ear, "Listen, you stupid bitch. I'm about sick of you. Get your sloppy, no-good snatch out of my bar before I call the cops." The same empty threat she heard every evening.

Splash!

"That's it!" he yelled.

The glass shattered on the floor, and Raven felt her arms being lifted over her shoulders.

"Stop it! Stop it!"

Startled customers looked on as the drunken woman was dragged outside.

"I don't wanna see you around here again. This time I mean it!"

Raven crawled on the sidewalk like a battered dog. Disgusted colonists stepped over her, treating her as a misplaced piece of human trash. The feeling was mutual. The dividing line between the rich and the poor grew wider every year. Raven had developed a sickening feeling of disdain for those in power. The promise of social equality was nothing more than a pipe dream fed to those willing to believe in it.

Except for a smashed box of cigarettes, Raven's pockets were empty. She'd spent her last Unics on shots and a needle of Mortis. Braving the weather, she raised her collar against the plummeting fall temperatures and maintained her composure as much as she could.

A silver-and-blue squad car crept by, and Raven felt the officers' intrusive bioscanner but avoided eye contact. Privacy was all but extinct with a government that took pride in bar coding its criminals for life.

A holographic banner soliciting votes for Governor Raul Batista for reelection held Raven's eyes as she crossed the busy intersection. After Raven beat the traffic light, her foot caught the inside of a drainage ditch. A sticky gunk oozed from her only pair of tennis shoes. Maybe she would steal another to replace them.

Her daily watering hole sat less than two blocks from a high-rise apartment complex in Emerald Colony.

She swiped the key card, and the glass slid open into a lavish foyer.

"Welcome home, Tiffany Raven," greeted an automated machine.

Another wasted day spent drowning out the past. And what made it worse was that she'd been awake only a little over three hours.

Raven passed the cracked door of an older married couple who'd recently moved in. They seemed to be arguing over something, but she couldn't tell what. A cruel thought entered her head: Raven contemplated telling the wife she'd fucked her husband while she was at work one night. There was some truth to it, but the midmorning session actually happened when the woman was at home. Another by-product of Raven's addiction to sex and alcohol.

The apartment was almost as bare as the day she'd leased it. She'd added hand-me-down furniture items from a thrift shop and a fridge full of empty takeout boxes and alcohol. Nothing extravagant like her neighbors. It kind of made her wonder how she ever afforded the place to begin with. The disability checks weren't enough to put food on the table and pay the rent. It had been a while since her last hunt, and money was tight. Raven figured walking the streets for a living might help her get by, if only to make enough to feed her vices. On second thought, perhaps a bullet was the better option.

Raven took a whiff of her armpits and then covered her nose. As usual, she'd forgotten to shower before leaving the house.

The water scalded Raven's fingers, turning her white flesh red. She preferred building up the steam to resemble a sauna. The apartment complex offered residents free access to a steam room, but Raven was self-conscious about her battle scars. She didn't want to entertain questions about the line running from her chest to her stomach. Telling the nosy neighbors she'd undergone open-heart surgery would just invite more questions.

Raven arched her back and soaped her long black hair with rose-scented shampoo. The loofah's softness felt good against her skin and breasts. She ran it to her legs and between her thighs. As Raven cleansed the buildup of two days' worth of foulness, she chuckled, pondering her evening schedule. *What schedule?* she thought.

After scrubbing her funky body, she'd probably try another bar and bargain a meal from some hormone-crazed college sap. If he was gullible enough, she could even get free drinks. Raven considered injecting the needle of Mortis she'd bought and spending the rest of the night high. At least then she wouldn't have to think. She wasn't expecting any calls or visitors, unless her neighbor admitted the affair to his wife. In Raven's screwed-up way of thinking, fighting was therapeutic. Kicking some broad's ass would liven her troubled spirits.

Like Raven's soul, her reflection was broken as she looked at herself in the foggy mirror. It had been seven years since Korea, and Raven felt she'd aged twice that number. She guessed she resembled what her mother would look like if they ever crossed paths. A sudden, brief sadness washed over Raven, but she shook it off. There was no time to grieve or show self-pity for growing up alone. In and out of juvenile detention since she was seven, Raven had opted for the JTF Marines in lieu of a ten-year sentence for grand larceny, and it had strengthened her character. Even if she was the poster child for what was wrong with the war's veterans.

Raven put on a fresh set of clothes, including a black tank top and blue capris, which fit snugly on her slender body. She topped off her outfit by pulling a warm white sweater over her head. She finished drying her hair and then lit a smoke out on the balcony.

A brilliant full moon illuminated the master bedroom and balcony as Raven gazed out on Emerald Colony. Against the beautiful backdrop of the Appalachian Mountains, the business district appeared exceptionally alive for this time of night. In the foreground, a rotorless police helicopter circled the Logan Museum of Space Exploration several blocks away. Whatever the occasion was, it did not concern Raven, who typically kept her distance from politics and the latest trends. She couldn't afford to vote and dressed as plainly as possible to avoid attention. Raven's instincts told her something big was going down at the museum, and she wanted no part of it.

Incoming assignment…Please confirm.

Raven couldn't believe her ears. A hunt? Her mind and body still struggling to recover from her midevening binge, Raven raced to her bed and retrieved her watch. A wondrous holographic display appeared, requesting her passcode. Raven typed *820404* onto the pad and waited for the system's response.

Hunter's identity confirmed. Please stand by for instructions.

Raven huffed impatiently, waiting for the details. She showed indifference, working for whoever paid her, and didn't ask questions. The generator of assignments was kept classified. Hunting was one of the few jobs she had been qualified for after leaving the service. Carrying a gun was an added bonus.

The hologram gave two solid beeps and then displayed the assignment's details. Suspected in the rape of a sixteen-year-old girl, a middle-aged male who went by the alias

Cherry_Popper13 was the target. The hunt was assigned for a measly three hundred Unics to kill on sight. Obviously the girl's family wasn't reporting it or leaving it up to the police to bring the pedophile to justice. And for good reason. The Emerald Colony Police Department was backlogged in investigations, and the force was stretched thin.

A sliding closet door revealed an assortment of weapons to choose from. Raven's personal favorite, the RK72, would sit this one out. She'd nearly caused unwarranted collateral damage on her last bounty, exposing more of the organization than those behind the screen cared for. The authorities saw a hunter as some sort of unregulated vigilante.

Hunts such as these were common after the courts had ruled high-school students at any age were capable of consenting to sex. This assignment would be easy money.

Raven used the encrypted watch she had code-named Orion to conduct a search of sex offenders in her district. Hundreds of profiles, ranging from doctors to the lowest of colonial scum, flashed on the hologram. Schoolteachers and notable public figures, who'd face defamation by their own doing, populated the list. No wonder the colony was on a rapid and continuous decline; not a soul could be trusted.

The Central Networking System (CNS) was police property. Whoever controlled the distribution of hunts must have sat high on the food chain for Raven to have access to such a privilege.

A previously convicted rotund-faced pervert, who'd been recently acquitted for the same damn thing, matched the description given in the assignment. The idiot wasn't even clever enough to put some effort into changing his virtual gaming name. He'd pleaded innocent on two occasions for lewd acts involving a minor, and it seemed the courts were turning a blind eye, which she expected of a corrupt judicial hierarchy. Raven guessed this stain on society was probably loaded or had some kind of pull. Either way, it was time he was paid a visit.

The black tactical vest did little to protect her from the icy winds. Raven could hear a pin drop a hundred yards away. She balanced her weight evenly on falling branches, hid in a light foggy haze, and used the thick bark for cover. Raven's swift feline tactics kept her movements concealed as she navigated the pitch-black forest. The dark visor highlighted a pack of indigenous life forms scouring the landscape for warm blood.

On the outskirts of the Farming District sat a luxurious two-story home surrounded by a seven-foot fence—cautious or just paranoid? Raven had been correct in her prejudgment. Two expensive cars sat parked in the driveway, and a third was underneath an open garage. Raven guessed the family might be asleep, as no lights or movement came from the home. This would prove beneficial to Raven, and she wouldn't have to kill him in front of his wife—not that she would care in his case.

Raven lobbed an EMP device over the fence into the back-yard. Within a matter of seconds, the weapon charged and disabled the home's security system. The dying safety lights in a heated pool let Raven know the device was functioning properly.

The smell of leaves and fresh-cut grass permeated the air. In Raven's peripheral vision, she could see a previously locked wooden shed. The red bar had given out shortly after the electrical disturbance, and Raven's curiosity was nagging her. She couldn't take her eyes off the structure. The same feeling she had felt before Captain Mallory kicked open that door crawled up her spine. Unseen horrors awaited within its walls, crying to be let out. The charge was good for forty-five minutes tops. More than enough time for a side investigation.

The handle jiggled loose in Raven's hand. She cut the pie inch by inch using the infrared connection between her visor and weapon. The darkness switched to a greenish tint as Raven surveyed the area. Raven's heart sank into her stomach when she saw what appeared before her.

Caged like animals, two naked college-age girls, who'd been bound and gagged, wiggled and grunted, begging to be freed. In the corner, a trough filled with pig slop had spilled over. A small cooler of brown water was festering with vermin. Without a second thought, Raven smashed the lock as hard as she could. She couldn't help but think of how scared Kim had been before the accident. Whatever sick and twisted god was playing this game of déjà vu surely was as demented as the man who'd kidnapped these girls. Her weapon's butt stock was of no use.

"Fuck it," Raven said under her breath. "Orion. Go silent."
Silenced mode selected.

A hole burned through the lock, and Raven used her foot to complete the job. One by one, she pulled the balls out of their swollen mouths. Mascara ran from the girls' eyes to their bruised and battered cheeks. Raven's boot squished a clump of human shit as she retrieved a knife from her ankle.

"Go," Raven told the girls. Freed from the confines of this hellish entrapment, the girls made a beeline for the double door. The heroic deed was short-lived, as just then Raven heard two gunshots come from the house. The flash of a muzzle gave away the target's location.

Silence mode deactivated...burst selected.

Raven navigated around the girls' dead bodies and discharged gunfire toward the second floor. No sooner than she'd created a hasty shooting position out of a table, her target returned the favor. This time he wasn't playing around. Raven listened to the cycling of a heavy weapon and escaped just in time, as it shredded her position into tiny pieces.

The sparks from Raven's barrel lit up her torso as she annihilated a side door and entered the home.

A suffocating billow of dust greeted Raven's face. Rotting human bodies, animal carcasses, and moldering furniture were a few of the amenities this creep had used to decorate the interior.

Raven's final day in Korea seemed to be on repeat. In a jar was the preserved head of a woman Raven presumed to be his wife. Crimson sporadically colored what used to be a white carpet. Contacting the police was out of the question. Raven had an assignment to complete, no matter what the cost.

She double-timed it to a staircase and prepped for a final assault. A hail of gunfire nearly took Raven's head off, lighting up the floorboards.

"When I'm done with you, I'll feed you to the whores I got hog-tied in the basement!" the man yelled in a slurred voice. He was so fat that Raven could hear the cheeseburgers blocking his windpipe.

She listened to him change belts and used it to her advantage by sending up a flash grenade.

"Aggh!"

A pulsating whitish glow filled the hallway. A partially loaded weapon was turned on its side as the smoke of spent rounds wafted from its hot barrel.

He'd retreated, but to where? There was no backup or calling for help. Unlike in Korea, Raven was on her own. She'd spent time on some tough assignments, but this was a nail biter. She felt the buildup of sweat under the visor making its way down her face.

Raven's vest pressed against the wall, and her weapon stayed low and ready. The house was bigger than she'd thought. An unexpected hallway added another obstacle.

The first door resisted Raven's left hand, but she kept her aim at twelve o'clock. The hinges tore off, and the wooden blockade slammed to the floor. Empty. Raven stopped herself from shouting the word "clear" out of habit. Had she teamed with another hunter, the dough would be split. Raven wasn't having any of that no matter how dangerous the assignments were.

Back into the hallway. The whale of a man was nowhere in sight. Raven's heart started racing, and the hair on the back of her neck stood up. A window at the end of the hallway, exposing a full moon, gave the house a gothic and ominous appearance. The sounds of the deceased haunted the attic above, seemingly in response to the heavy winds beating on the house.

*Dong...dong...*Raven's eyes followed the weapon to the rear. Nothing but a rusty clock on its last leg.

Raven was faced with a command decision that could cost her her life. Two doors opposed each other. One cracked, the other fully shut. Raven was running out of time, and she started for the shut door but then turned for the other. Her hesitation was a grave mistake. The wood split in half, and he pinned Raven's arms to her side. Her weapon was flung out of her hands as her body crashed into the opposing door.

Raven felt as if she had been crushed under a tipped-over cow. His wet tongue slurped her chin and cheekbones.

"You're the prettiest one yet."

Raven's legs drifted apart as he undid his buckle.

"I don't think so."

The man screamed out in pain from Raven's boot blade. Red blood and bile from a pierced organ spurted from his backside. The world lifted off Raven's chest, and she gasped for air. She somersaulted to her feet and roundhouse-kicked her target, slicing the blade into his thick neck.

He gurgled and coughed up his insides. Raven wasn't done. This jerk-off had tried to rape her. The same way he had raped...*the prettiest one yet?* Who was this blob of fat talking about? Had there been other hunters before her? Asking him wouldn't help, since he was bleeding to death from a slashed throat. Raven dug deeper into his larynx. Her blade met bone and cartilage, digging and cutting deeper into her kill. His bloody spasm came to a halt, his pupils enlarged, and his eyes rolled into the back of his head.

Raven's blade collapsed, and she watched his decapitated head roll off his torso. Fifteen minutes remained on the charge.

"Orion. Upload target's identification."

A blue funnel emitted from Raven's wrist and started at the dead man's feet. The visor kept track of the percentage of the match and relayed it back to Raven. The butterflies started moving in her stomach, and she held her breath. Though this wasn't her first rodeo, the final confirmation still caused her a bit of worry. Without a 100 percent match, the hunt would be classified as a homicide. Raven had never made such a rookie mistake, even in her training days, which was why she chose to work alone. Less chance for error.

Upload complete...Stand by for confirmation...100 percent match.

Homer A. Turner, senior accountant for the Lunar Crystal Corporation, lay dead in his home, along with several woman who'd gone missing. Or had they? Raven's first thought was the money. She'd been paid peanuts to take out a high-priority target. The second thought was that the women all shared one characteristic. Could've been a sick fetish of Homer's, but all the girls were of Central American descent.

Raven ran a bioscan of two dead Latinas in the living room, with negative results. Either they'd been born and bred for this kind of treatment, or they'd had their identities erased by someone with the technology and power to do so.

———

Raven gripped the headboard with one hand and placed the other on Will's waist. Each throbbing thrust sent Raven closer to orgasm, and she moaned in a state of erotic ecstasy. His palms held Raven's glistening torso, and she backed into Will's cock at a quick and even pace.

"Give me that big, black, juicy dick, baby. Give it to me."

The smacking of wet genitals and smell of animalistic sex elevated her senses. She jiggled Will's ball sack in her fingers, inviting him to ejaculate deep and hard. Raven clenched her toes and let out a loud cry as Will filled her hot pussy.

The soaked pillow welcomed her face, and she squeezed the last drops of semen from Will's cock. Her lover went flaccid and plopped next to her.

"Whew. Damn. You sure do know how to make a girl cum."

Before Will could respond, Raven leaned over and gave Will a long kiss and caressed his shrunken member. For the first time since she could remember, Raven felt a trickle of passion. Sure, Will was married, but Raven wasn't able to control herself. Ever since her first night with Will, she had wanted more of him. She'd cut back on one-night stands, hoping to catch Will away from Deborah. Raven's lack of a strong male figure in her life was partly responsible for her distorted view of what was acceptable in terms of forming a healthy relationship with the opposite sex.

The bedsheets came undone as Will said, "You gotta go before Deborah gets here."

"Sure thing," replied Raven, with a halfhearted salute in Will's direction. As he got dressed, Raven admired Will's muscular body.

"That means now, Tiffany."

Raven yawned and twisted herself out of bed. "Right."

It was nearly lunchtime, and Deborah was due to come home any minute. Will mentioned that Deborah was getting a head start on Thanksgiving dinner, and they were expecting family. Raven never cared for the holidays much. After the military, holiday meals consisted of Wild Turkey and a bag of Chinese takeout, if that.

Raven slipped on the running outfit and beanie she'd come over in and gave Will a final kiss. She checked both sides of the hallway and slowly closed the door. A puzzled expression formed on a young boy's face as he watched Raven leave the apartment. The boy's eyes followed Raven as she made her way to the elevator. *Mind your own business, you little shit*, she wanted to tell the snoopy brat. But doing so might hurt his feelings, and he would tell his parents, who'd come looking for her to apologize. Raven reserved no sympathy for children. The world was a cruel son of a bitch, and they'd find out sooner or later.

"Scoot," Raven shooed in a hushed voice. School must've let out early, or the boy wouldn't be hanging around the apartment-complex hallways, prying into other people's personal lives.

"Get in here!" hollered a man of medium stature. Red sauce was spilled on his shirt, and he'd armed himself with a steel rod. Like an obedient house pet, the kid followed his guardian's command, keeping his head down and his hands in his pockets. He never spoke a word. When he reached the threshold, the frizzle-haired man whacked the boy's head and threw the door closed. Whip after whip, scream after scream, Raven listened to the man beat the kid remorselessly.

Don't get involved. Take your own advice and mind your business. Raven's inner rage and code of silence fought with each other. The whimpers of the boy trailed off into another room. She got one foot off the ground as the elevator opened, but she was caught off guard by a woman on the other side of the door. Deborah's arms were stretched from the bags of groceries she was struggling to keep intact.

The African American woman paid no heed to Raven and rolled her eyes when she moved aside to let her by.

Bitch.

An intoxicating scent of expensive perfumed followed Deborah, and her clothes were top of the line. The wireless key in Deborah's purse allowed her to enter the apartment with relative ease.

I can see why Will hates her, thought Raven as the elevator made its descent. The entitled gold digger had married

Will only for his money and seemed the type to beat feet when the well ran dry. She swore the next time that cunt disrespected her, she'd give her something to swallow other than a cock.

The previous night had given Raven an overdue reality check; she recognized that her speed and endurance lacked significantly. She tightened her laces and flexed her joints. The morning was bitter cold, but a light jog before turning in might help her sleep.

Raven picked a quiet path behind the apartment and set out. A breathtaking view of the sun shining off skyscrapers redirected her attention from her sore calves. She'd never realized just how beautiful Emerald Colony was. She took in the aroma of fallen leaves and fresh food emitting from a hot-dog stand. An elderly couple sat together on a bench, not speaking yet keeping close. Raven envisioned this was part of a ritual: two colonists who'd raised children and were spending their remaining years together, sitting every morning in the park. She wasn't one for romance but couldn't help but feel for the two. She wondered if her own parents, who'd abandoned her, somewhere comforted each other, regretting their decision to leave a child to fend for herself.

The trail veered to the right, and Raven was not ready to quit. A waterfall of perspiration soaked her outfit, but overall she felt good. Amazing, actually. Ignoring the pain, Raven increased the pace. She huffed and puffed. After seeing a senior colonist's decorated hat, she felt a surge of patriotism;

five miles a day was the minimum in boot camp. Raven's feet ached, and her back wanted to seize up, but she wasn't stopping. She fixated on a statue of Governor Elaine Banks, Emerald Colony's founder, and sprinted. The nearly two-hundred-year-old bronze structure beckoned her to make the same sacrifices as those before her—to do whatever it takes.

A cyclist made his way on the path and pushed to the grass. Raven's soles tore, and a merciless gust fought hard to knock her over. She finished by leaping over an imaginary line and inhaled what she swore to be ice. She returned the cyclist's nod and panted so rapidly he almost stopped to help.

"I'm fine," said Raven, waving him off.

She fell on her knees to catch herself and hawked a glob of spit. She wanted to go for two more miles, but they'd come at a price she wasn't ready to pay. Her cranium wanted to explode, and everything around her was moving in different directions all at the same time. Cursing herself for improper pacing, she squatted for a moment—a bad idea. After realizing this, she hopped to her feet. *It is definitely time for new shoes.*

"Shit," said Raven. The trail was starting to bustle, and there were too many colonists to view the assignment's details in private.

Raven hustled toward a restroom, past a runner who obviously yearned to relieve himself.

"Sorry. I have to go really bad. I'll be quick," she told him, shutting the door to the unisex restroom. She twisted the lock and ignored the man's obscenities. The eyes of a red dragon, which had been spray-painted on the wall, penetrated the very fabric of Raven's psyche. The symbol, the likes of which she'd never seen, appeared extremely unsettling, as if threatening her existence. Sometime, somewhere soon, Raven knew she and the symbol would meet again.

God's Wrath

Those fortunate enough to survive the fire reclaimed their fallen home. The flames had reduced the shelter to nothing but ashes spread across a concrete jungle. A malnourished woman who hadn't bathed in ages cradled a newborn in a dirty blanket. Blazes brought to light the solemn faces of a group huddled around a trash can. The ground was littered with colonists wrapped in sleeping bags, their vital signs drastically diminished. By the end of winter, most would be dead from hypothermia, starvation, or worse.

Raven felt the despair, regret, and hatred that were ever present among the colonists. Betrayed by those who had sworn to protect them. Betrayed by God himself. Their bodies trembled in fear, afraid she was there to take them away. Who would do this kind of thing—murder people who'd asked for help? All hope extinguished with the flick of a match.

A young man watched Raven's every move from the corner of his eye. His vitals were strong, and the look of guilt was written all over his face.

"Orion. Confirm target." The invisible eye visor stopped at 25 percent. She needed to get closer. "Stand still, you son of a bitch." The man wasn't waiting around to find out whether Raven was ECPD or not.

Her concealed side arm poked at her rib cage as she raced around the slumbering colonists. The man broke left into an alley, but Raven was quick to keep up. Nervous, he stumbled over a grate in an attempt to reach the fire escape. *They* wanted him dead, but she needed him alive. He abandoned his fire-escape plan and tried to outrun her. Commending herself for not indulging in her usual remedies, Raven closed in. Unless he possessed the agility to scale a ten-foot fence, he was shit out of luck. To Raven's surprise, he was actually stupid enough to try.

They rolled to the ground, and she gripped his dome in a headlock, pressing the gun's barrel into his temple.

"Orion…confirm…target," said Raven, catching her breath.

"You ain't got nuttin' on me. Let me go. You ain't even a real cop," he cried.

"No, I'm not a cop, but trust me. I'm a lot worse." She gave him some breathing room and stood up. She pushed him once again and said, "Now, tell me what you know…Tyrone."

"I ain't talking to no bitch acting like she got a badge."

"Fine, then. Either way, I get paid." Raven centered the laser from her sound-suppressed pistol on Tyrone's forehead.

"Yo! What the fuck!"

"Listen here. You have five seconds."

"All right! Get dat gun out my face!"

She honored Tyrone's request and holstered the weapon under her jacket. "Start talking."

Tyrone walked back and forth, and his eyes started to moisten. "He made me do it. He told me I would get my cut of the money. He ain't gave me shit!"

Another industrial-district colonist used for personal gain. Young and gullible. Raven, not too long ago, had been in Tyrone's shoes.

"You're not very convincing. The clock's still ticking," said Raven, reaching for her side arm.

"I already—"

"Who? Who put you up to this?"

A waterfall surged from Tyron's eyes, and his mouth quivered.

"Last chance, Tyrone."

"It wasn't supposed to go down like dat."

"Three…"

"Come on, man!"

"Two…"

Tears still streaming.

"Time's up!"

"Julio. Julio. I swear it was his idea. I'm gonna kill dat nigga."

She lowered the pistol and said, "You just cost me a whole lot of money."

Raven suspected Tyrone didn't have the audacity to willingly burn down a homeless shelter without being coerced. Still, if she didn't take him out, someone soon enough would.

"How much?" she asked.

"Huh?"

"Don't play stupid. How much did he promise?"

"Five Gs."

"You're gonna tell me exactly where I can find him." She'd broken protocol and was far outside her realm.

"He one of dem big-time niggas. Come down here all decked out. Tossing cash like it grow on trees and shit."

"You're trying my patience."

"Dat fool gotta be BD."

"Speak English."

"Blood Dragon. There, I said it. Now can I go?"

Blood Dragon? Raven was aware of most gangs in Emerald Colony, but this one eluded her memory. The moment Tyrone uttered the words, she thought back to the symbol in the restroom. Whichever thugs were responsible for the fire were trying to make a name for themselves and weren't afraid to take the lives of others to do so.

"Leave town, Tyrone."

"I ain't got nowhere to go."

"That's not my problem, now, is it?"

A botched hunt wasn't going to go over well. Raven figured her actions would result in termination. Perhaps literally.

She accessed Orion and sent a code to Ops relaying that she'd lost the target. It would buy her more time.

A sleek black sports car homed in on Raven's position and stopped halfway. Tyrone took a step back, observing the weaponized and armored vehicle.

The engine revved, and Raven drove away, leaving Tyrone behind.

"Orion. Scan Central for a Julio including possible ties to Blood Dragons."

A torrential icy downpour blanketed the colony. She traveled alone, zipping through the industrial district. Cops were few and far between in this part of the colony. An array of abandoned buildings and barred shops lined the streets. Harlots stood under an overhang, waiting out the storm.

Scan complete. Stand by for findings.

"Now we're getting somewhere."

Orion locked on to the bar code of a paroled convict who'd served a light sentence for embezzlement.

Confined three years for fraud? The stench of venality was so strong she could almost taste it.

A picture in Julio's profile showed a tattoo of a red dragon across his backside.

"My, my, will you look at that."

Raven could've easily turned back, killed Tyrone, uploaded his vitals, and lined her pockets, but someone had to pay for what had happened. Tyrone was the fall guy, an expendable pawn, sacrificed by a player who held the winning hand.

Raven tightened her fist around the steering wheel and increased her speed. She pictured men, women, and children burning and screaming, just as she had seen helpless Koreans roasted alive at the hands of a tyrannical government.

St. Paulina's Catholic Church was possessed by a demon, and Raven was the exorcist.

Miniature candles flickered in the chilly draft as the double door creaked open. Upon his cross, a somber Christ condemned this walking sin to hell. Bittersweet, she'd come to cast the first stone.

In the face of Lilith, a startled worshiper fled from the pews into the night. The signal had led Raven to the priest's sacristy. Julio didn't strike her as an altar boy. And she wasn't getting her hopes up that he'd changed overnight.

Robes hung from the racks, and a Bible sat on a table next to an empty wine glass. Raven's intuition had failed her before, but Orion was a damn-near error-proof AI system.

"Orion. Relocate."

From behind her, a click.

Raven kept her hands up and remained still. Her weapon was yanked from her fingers and flung to the ground.

"You've got some real nerve coming around here." The smell of must and pine filled Raven's nose to the point she wanted to gag.

"Has anyone ever told you that you smell *really* bad?"

"This white bitch got jokes. Laugh at this."

Raven's lower back caved in from a kick, and Julio's hand circled around her throat. He slammed her skull into the wall, and a framed picture of the Virgin Mary shattered on the floor. Her face felt like it was turning blue, and her heartbeat slowed down. Julio's words were clouded, and Raven's vision turned into less than a haze.

Each strenuous effort to break free was met with violent resistance. She crossed her hands on her chest, leaned over, and coughed up a lung. He smashed her face against the table with brute force, breaking it apart and cracking her jaw.

"That little snitch of yours is swimming up the Mississippi."

The weight of a table leg stung Raven's back, denying her attempt to raise herself up. Over and over, she endured Julio's merciless onslaught. Her arms gave out, and Julio left her sprawled amid the wreckage.

Get up, Raven. Get...up.

"You know, you're kind of cute," said Julio, twirling Raven's weapon. "Ah, who needs this old thing? I got me a new toy."

Raven's leg wobbled like Jell-O, and her hair was matted to her forehead. Julio's childlike grin stretched from ear to ear. Beads of perspiration covered the dragon etched into his skin.

"I've got friends in high places, *chica*. Friends that'll put you away for good."

Raven wasn't saying any prayers looking down the barrel of her gun.

"Before I kill you...tell me something." Raven's mind-fucking self-assurance threw Julio for a loop. "Why?"

Julio stomped and twisted the weapon. He bit his lip and put one foot forward. "You one stupid cracker-ass dyke. You think *I* killed those people?"

"Of course not. You're a man of God. An ordained priest, right? Father Mendez."

"Suck my—"

"Using displaced colonists to do your bidding. Not much has changed, has it? Batting for the devil now, I see."

"You don't know shit!"

Raven had Julio right where she wanted.

"This is my house! My rules!"

A drop of blood from her mouth landed next to her shoe. She wiped the runoff on her sleeve. "You know what they say—follow the money."

Raven put the final nail in the coffin. Eight thousand volts of lunar-crystal current flowed from Julio's wrist into a spider effect throughout the rest of his body. He burned to a skeletal crisp and buckled to the ground.

Raven scattered Julio's ashes and said, "Tell your *God* I said hi."

With her hand stopped at her watch, she lowered her head and took a deep breath. Her options were limited. Raven never failed an assignment and wasn't rushing to admit she'd veered out of her lane.

She watched the remnants of Julio's charred skull give in and crumble. She couldn't help but feel the same, watching him disintegrate.

The rabbit hole ran deeper than this. It had to. There was no denying it. Julio had taken one for the team, though he was unaware he'd been sacrificed. Besides, Julio had had it coming. She'd tailed and executed one of the clergy for a hit-and-run that had occurred a few years back, except it had been no accident. The victim was to testify against Julio, who had wasted parish resources to fund an all-expenses-paid vacation to the

Philippines. Raven knew how the story ended, long after the fact. This time, blood was on his hands. Julio's picture might have appeared under the definition of "scam artist," but he was no killer, at least not by dictionary standards.

Raven listened to the voice in the back of her head. Accessing Orion's AI system, she aborted the assignment.

Why did I not just shoot him and go home? She ripped Orion off her wrist and started for the exit.

Abortion rejected. Neutralize target.

"What? Orion, abort the assignment. Tyrone is dead, and I'm pulling out."

Opting for a more reliable signal, Raven used Orion to hack Joint Space Agency satellites. She searched the length of the Mississippi River for Tyrone's bar code. His beacon was dropping in depth. Before she lost him, Raven ordered, "Orion. Vital status. Now."

Stand by. Confirming vitals. Subject deceased.

"Orion. Upload Tyrone's vitals to Ops. Do it!" commanded Raven.

Abortion rejected. Neutralize target.

Orion contravened Raven's command when she sent up Julio's status.

Abortion reject—

"Silent!" Raven ordered.

Endless papers, most dating back decades, were dispersed throughout each desk in the sacristy. Business transactions, construction orders, illegible laundry receipts, none of them organized. "Think, damn it."

She turned her attention to an unsecure computer terminal on Julio's desk. She extracted data files containing communications from insurance brokers and the colony's southern port security. Raven's heart nearly stopped when she came across the images of naked Latin Americans blindfolded and caged in a military facility.

———

An obnoxious emcee and the procession of a high-school band, playing Emerald's national anthem, "I Will Survive," gave Raven a migraine headache.

The pillow wasn't working, and the earbuds weren't compatible with her disk player. "Arrgh." Twisting and turning, she drew the blanket over her hair.

"Here's to a one hundred and seventy-six Thanksgiving. Give it up for the West Emerald High School Ensemble," blared the emcee.

"Yeah!"

"Woooo!"

"That's my son!"

"Everybody sing along! I've got all my life to give…"

"Shut up! I'm trying to sleep, for crying out loud!" Raven wanted to shove that mic down his larynx and pop every balloon on stage. "I hate that song," she muttered.

She massaged her tender neck and cracked her knuckles. Her fingers left white imprints on her purple ankle. Raven imagined that this must be what it would feel like to get hit by an eighteen-wheeler. Her profession didn't provide medical coverage, and an eviction notice loomed in the near future. She'd gotten in over her head, and the bill was quite expensive.

The distress was too much to bear. Handicapped, Raven picked her least damaged extremity and hop-skipped to the bioregenerator.

"So much for that new pair of shoes."

Raven's left arm took an eternity to find its place, and her leg popped, flattening—

"Oh my..."

Happy Thanksgiving, Tiffany, greeted a male, British-accented artificial-intelligence nanny. *How are you doing this splendid morning?*

"Ahh...geez...ahh."

Tiffany?

"Just get on with it...whew."

I see you're in pain.

"No, Francis. I'm feeling super-duper today."

Should I cancel the regeneration?

She'd purchased the cheapest nanny on the market and dreaded its black-and-white communication system. She'd established a love-hate relationship with Francis and favored upgrading his capacity. A mind trapped in a machine was a terrible thing to waste. How anyone could subject himself to such a life was beyond her comprehension.

"Negative."

Very well.

Paralyzed from the neck down, she let out a sigh of relief as the comforting oceanic blue radiated on her skin.

I am detecting minor damage to several critical components.

"Really?"

That is affirmative. Would you like me to list them?

"Yes, Francis. Please tell me why I feel like I'm going to die."

I can assure you that your injuries are not life threatening.

She'd be better off talking to a wall. "Francis…"

As you wish.

Torn lower back muscle, dislocated…

"Francis, just put me at full health."

The AI's voice trailed off into a scarcely audible whisper.

———

What you got there? Oh, it's so beautiful.

Look, Mommy. I did it all on my own.

Yeah! You're such a big girl. I love you so, so much.

Hehehe. Stop. You're tickling me. Hehehe.

That's you…and that's me and Daddy.

Why is my hair blue?

I don't know. Hehehe.

Mommy.

Yes.

Peekaboo. Hehehe.

I see you too.

Hehehe.

Bye, sweetie.

Mommy, where are you going?

...

Mommy, come back!

...

No! Mommy, come back. No! Mommy!

Come on! Here's a couple bucks.

That's a good girl...take it in all the way.

You've got...ugh...some natural talent.

Stick with me...ugh, right there, baby...and there's a lot more where this came from.

No, no. Finish it...ugh...swallow all of it...there ya go...

You're not gonna last a second.

Go ahead. Report me. See if I give a fuck. We're all gonna die anyway.

You wanna find an accessible vein.

What do you mean? Cunt, you're gonna pay for this on your back.

Scream, bitch. Let it out. You're just making this harder than it has to be.

I take you in, feed you, and clothe you, and you can't show the tiniest grain of gratitude.

Damn kid!

Get back here.

You're gonna learn to respect your elders.

Nice and tight. Just the way I like it.

I'm sorry, but you don't qualify without a college education.

We ain't hiring.

I don't hire veterans. Too much liability.
You're gonna have to beg on your knees if you want a hit.
Now, bark.
Sit.
Roll over.
Spread your legs.
Good girl.

———

A fifth of rum dropped to the carpet, crushing empty beer cans. Raven's eyes were bloodshot, and her wet hair was frizzled.

The night lamp nailed the wall, sending the apartment into darkness, and the disk player broke into pieces. Raven flipped the mattress over and helplessly buckled. She pouted uncontrollably, pounding her fists into the ground. What happened next sent her over the edge of insanity.

Raven's fury was fueled by the sound of the parental discipline coming from within the walls. With blood boiling, she raised up.

"That's it, motherfucker."

After almost locking herself out the armory, she selected a cannon of a pistol. Raven bashed open the apartment door and saw double.

She didn't wait for an invitation. A digitized naked female masturbated on a screen by the couch, and a half-eaten plate of turkey and dressing rested on a coffee table. The dog cage was a reminder of what she'd come for.

She forced the bedroom door wide open, and what she saw sustained her anger. Raven stopped him in midair of his umpteenth strike as the guardian's hair became entangled in her grasp. Kicking and screaming, he raked his fingernails against the wallpaper. Raven dragged him into the living room, and the dark-skinned boy shadowed her there, confused as to what he'd done.

She implanted the guardian's face into his dinner not once but twice, three, four times. In a fit of rage, she bashed his head in with no remorse. Blood splattered on Raven's face, and the boy stood in shock, watching his oppressor dealt a taste of his own medicine.

An unintelligible utterance came from the man's smashed mouth, but Raven ignored it. A spew of thick gore and loosened teeth poured out.

"If you ever touch him again, I will kill you."

The weapon she jabbed into him added insult to injury when he tried to talk. "I speak; you listen. Got me, asshole? You have one of two options."

Raven relished the power she held over this abusive animal.

"You leave Emerald tonight on your own, or I'll give you a first-class ticket out the window."

"Ye…yes."

"Yes, what?"

"Yes, ma'am, I'll leave."

She'd get two years minimum for this drunken assault, but she wasn't counting on seeing his face again. One final kick to bring the point home.

Raven looked at the boy. "You're coming with me."

She saw he was dressed in the same tattered and torn clothes as the day prior. His cheekbones poked through his skin, and threads hung out his moccasins.

"*Vamos a ir!*"

Hearing his native tongue, Raven sucked in her waist and said, "Yeah, yeah. Let's go before I change my mind."

I see we have a visitor. His embedded identification is missing. Would you like me to notify the district police?

"What?"

I see we—

"Francis, I heard you the first time."

The remaining cleaning bot finished brushing the lamp and disk player before scooting into a cupboard. The boy's legs shivered; he hadn't moved an inch since coming in. Raven grunted, closing the window, and said, "*Sentarse!*"

Too weak to make it across the room, he crawled to the remade bed and lay down.

She was at a loss for words and put Orion on the nightstand. Like the women Homer had raped and murdered, the kid's identity had been wiped without a trace. The boy's highwater pants revealed a deep incision, and Raven felt a wetness under his clothes.

He became squeamish in her arms and tried, unsuccessfully, to pull loose.

"Stop squirming." A little hand slapped across Raven's face, and she locked in his wrist.

The boy screamed and screamed, "*Dejame ir*," and nearly broke his own arm before Raven was able to adjust the ankle locks. She put the last arm in place and hit the close button.

She could see dislodged and rotten teeth behind a silently wailing open mouth.

"Francis, full health," said Raven, blowing a circle of smoke.

Please be advised that your bank account will have a balance of ten remaining Unics if you proceed.

"I'll worry about that later. Fix 'em up."

The boy's struggling died down, and soon he was out cold.

———

One of two beastly bouncers hid the Unics in his rear pocket. A blast of bass-heavy rap music filled the warehouse and then became muffled.

The taller one's stare began at Raven's feet and ended at her cleavage. He asked, "You here for ladies' night, or do you need a room?"

"What's it gonna cost me?"

"We're charging two hundred. You get seventy-five percent, and the rest goes to the house."

"I'll take it."

"Room one oh two. Checkout is at noon."

She slipped the key card into her black stocking as the bar was pushed down from steroid-induced strength.

The rooms looked and sounded like a living cesspool of debauchery. A twentysomething in pigtails and a school outfit had one hand on her hip and was chomping on pink bubblegum. Banging and moaning sounded from behind closed doors.

"Nice," complimented a spent male heading for the steam room. Some ladies sneered at Raven and retreated into their rooms, jealous she'd take the lion's share of customers.

Raven saw the lips of a black girl slobbering on a chunky Asian's dick through a glory hole. *Must be here for ladies' night*, she thought.

Despite the overall atmosphere of a modern-day Sodom and Gomorrah, Raven's room was tidy and noticeably lacking the malodor of stale jizz. She hung up her leather trench coat, lay back on the satin sheets, and crossed her legs. A small red light came on, and the door slid open.

"Don't talk," said Raven, using one finger to beckon Will. Horny and hot for his dark mistress, Will dropped his pants and arched his back. Raven's black lips parted, and her mouth filled with Will's hard cock. She circled her tongue on the bottom, slowly pumping his shaft. No gag reflex stopped her swallowing him whole as she felt the mushroom on her tonsils.

Her nostrils inhaled Will's musk as she sucked on his genitals. Will's nut sack swirled in her mouth, and her soft hand lubricated his dick in saliva. The eroticism had Raven's pussy begging for him to take her.

"Baby...your mouth is fantastic."

"I want you inside me," said Raven, leaning back on the bed. Will took the lead and climbed between Raven's thighs.

"Ooh...put it in me," she moaned, as Will's tip gently touched her sensitive clit.

Back and forth he rammed into Raven's hungry cunt. With one heel on his buttocks and the other in the air, she held on tightly to her manly stud.

"Fuck me…fuck me…I wanna feel it…harder!"

"I'm cumming…you're so hot."

"Fill this pussy up. Fuck yeah."

Raven clawed Will's back and crossed her legs. He suckled on her exposed sweaty nipple and pumped faster. In a state of primal lust, Raven pulled in Will's pelvis, savoring the blast of goodness deep into her hole.

"Tiffany, damn baby."

Raven wanted more and even thought of roaming the halls for more cock, but there were more pressing issues.

They rolled over, and Will slipped his forearm over his forehead as she rested on his heaving broad chest and shoulders. It wasn't very romantic, listening to a couple fuck next door. But Raven had gotten what she wanted—or more like needed after what she'd been through. A rough sexing was just what the doctor ordered. But in truth, she'd come for something else. And now was as good a time as any.

While her lover lay in bed, Raven got up to light a blunt.

"I can't; my wife will kill me."

Persuading Will to dip out had been difficult enough, let alone what she'd asked him to bring.

"She thinks I'm at the office." Believable, if it weren't Thanksgiving weekend.

Raven's plate was full, but not of turkey dinner. Could Will be trusted, or was he like the rest of the men in her life? Manipulative, until they got her in bed. She'd soon get her answer. Club Sodom was the only place they were safe. Concerned with getting off, nobody there would second-guess the two.

Raven sound-suppressed the room using a switch and asked, "Where is it?"

"I'd knew you'd ask. Check my pants."

A condom he didn't need, a seventy-five Unic bill (which she stuffed into her bra), and there…there it was.

"Everything you asked for."

Raven studied the data chip and said, "Will, I owe you."

"Don't worry about it. I had to get away. I can listen to my father-in-law's war stories only so many times. I know the lines better than he does."

He had risked a lucrative career at WAR, and Raven had lured him with the raunchy sex that Deborah failed to provide under normal circumstances—not to mention the twice-a-month limit his wife imposed when preparing for photo shoots.

"What'd you name him?"

"Took a minute to think of one, but I settled on Enrico."

Expecting Will to get dressed with her, she watched as he tied a towel around his waist. She held no resentment. An adult of his status should enjoy himself. She'd locked away a few skeletons of her own. Perhaps more.

"I won't wait up."

Judgment by Fire

———◆———

FOR A SECOND she thought she'd spent the night at Will's, until little Enrico joined in and imitated the buzz-haired anime hero defeating a green alien. The apartment smelled of hazelnut coffee, bacon, and eggs.

The loud holovision set made Raven thankful she'd been born infertile, and she made a mental note to move her bed into the bedroom. So he wouldn't miss the scenes from next week's episode, Enrico ran into the kitchen during a commercial and fixed his plate. The software in his data chip allowed seamless translation for all known languages, freeing Raven from having to use broken Spanish. He'd also been given the ability to speak any language.

She discarded the empty chip into a drawer, and...

"Enrico?"

The preteen turned to look at her and smiled.

"Be a good little boy and give me back Ori...my watch."

Spilling orange juice everywhere, he ran through the apartment, giggling all the way to his room.

She chased after Enrico in her pajamas and said, "This isn't funny, you little runt."

Raven playfully wrestled him on the king-size bed but put in a bit of elbow grease to pry Orion off his arm.

"It doesn't fit you anyway. I'll get you one, one day, but for now..."

Raven stumbled, her feet cold with spilled juice, and she lifted Enrico up before he could ruin anything else.

"Stop running through the rooms. There are people still asleep."

"OK."

Raven was taken aback, hearing Enrico speak English for the first time.

"You stay here and watch your cartoons. Don't turn to channel—"

Raven snatched the remote and blocked out all adult entertainment. "Don't answer the door under any circumstances, and stay away from..."

She locked the armory and alarmed it. "Is that understood?"

"No problemo." His little legs snapped together, and a flattened hand raised to his eyebrow.

"Scram, sailor boy. I got work to do."

Raven cracked the door to her study to listen in for any trouble Enrico might cause. Orion connected to the computer system and uploaded the latest files extracted from the comm link.

"All right, Julio, let's see what you were hiding," said Raven, hitting play on the computer.

Father Mendez, I take it you've considered my offer by now?

I've thought about it.

You'll be paid in full when the job is done.

I heard that the last time.
Good, so you're in.
Yeah...
There was a pause.
I'm game.
And the patsy?
Some thug holed up there.
Gotta love 'em.
Hey...
There was a longer pause.
Don't forget who's in control here, Julio.
What about—
Your passport will be waiting.
And the—
Cash in hand.
Thank you, Father.
May God be with you.

She brought one knee up and rested her elbow on it. The ashtray caught the flicks from her butt as she waited for the extensive search to complete. She couldn't resist checking over her shoulder every now and then, partly expecting Enrico to show her what mischief he'd gotten himself into.

Raven swiped the window aside and played another file to save time.

Julio, man. I think the cops are on to you.
What you talking about, J. Dog?
That little snitch was running his mouth to ECPD.
I knew it. Handle that shit.

Consider it done.

"J. Dog, huh?" Raven crushed the cigarette under her fingers, and she maximized the first zipped file. Orion wasn't any help—87 percent, some 99, but none a perfect match.

A sobering wail came from Enrico's room, and Raven, in her suppressed motherly instinct, ran out of the study. The holovision was on a restricted screen, and the armory's keypad flashed red.

On his bed, Enrico lay curled in the fetal position, bawling his eyes out. Her newfound appendix hadn't come with instructions, so Raven chose her words carefully.

"Enrico? What's the matter?" asked Raven, trying her damnedest to be nice.

"Bad man…coming to get me."

Raven clenched her fist and then exhaled, her eyes widening, realizing what he'd just said.

She didn't think interrogating Enrico would prove effective, so she gave it the kinder, gentler approach. He sniffled and trembled in her arms. The good news or the bad news? There was no bad news. No way in hell was she going to let anyone take Enrico away from her.

"Enrico, no one's coming; I promise you."

"The bad man said so. I heard him."

"What bad man?" Enrico's sniffling became intermittent, and she ran her thumb under his eyes.

"The man who brought me here."

With one squeeze of the trigger, the man's head exploded. The remaining hostages sat bound, chair to chair. Two empty shells bounced on the floor and then settled in a pool of blood.

"One of y'all better start talking," said Jermaine, flanked by his suited thugs. "We'll go over this again."

A sharply dressed Asian woman who'd sustained a busted nose gasped, staring into the twelve-gauge.

"My associates have informed me we're short sixty million Unics." The cornrow-haired boss cocked the barrel and asked, "You wouldn't know anything about this, would you?"

The man shook his head, mute.

"Fifty thousand a pop. Is that so much to ask for?"

Jermaine duck walked in open-ranks fashion and said to the next, "If you're following the rules, why are any of you sitting here? I should be balls deep in some ass."

"I was gonna put it back," cried a hostage.

"Ah. We have a winner."

A henchman brought out the confessor's wife and had her kneel. Hands collapsed in prayer, she pleaded, "Kevin! Please, we only—"

Bam! Kevin screamed, and the others turned from Jermaine's barbaric display of discipline.

The henchmen lined up with rifles aimed at all the hostages. Jermaine never intended leaving any witnesses. As far as he was concerned, they were *all* guilty of playing him for a fool. If she didn't act now, it would be too late.

Three choking-gas canisters shot over the railing into the factory. The men gagged and dispersed behind cover.

Raven shifted her aim away from the hostages' green out-
lines to a henchman's spine. Her position was rocked with a
blast of shells, protruding from the metal board. She held the
upper terrain but was outnumbered.

Jermaine was priority number one. His blue designator
was absent amid the thick mist as Raven crept in silence.

Blood gushed from the throat of a butch woman who'd
separated from the pack. Three to one.

"I always knew you'd come for me!" called out Jermaine,
hidden within the gray cloud. "But, you see, I can't be
caught."

Snipe! A bullet pinged off the pipe, and the cartridge hit
the ground.

"I know all about your kind!" His voice was everywhere at
once. "Taking the law into your own hands! Snuffing out the
bad guys. A real fucking hero of the day!"

The man's neck twisted, and he was eased down. Raven
aimed high and then low as the smoke started to clear.

"Look left," warned Jermaine.

Raven's visor cracked open, and her legs swept up. Coming
down hard on her back, she escaped the follow-up and spun to
into a fight stance. Inches away from point-blank range, the
bullet hit the ceiling, and Jermaine tore both the RK72 and
sling from her body. The weapon slid across the floor, stopping at the hostages.

Raven was forced off balance by Jermaine's spin kick, but
he missed his mark. He was slow to block Raven's counter and
was clocked cold in the face. The buttons on his suit jacket

popped, and his dress shirt tore. Jermaine, sporting a cut physique, threw his fist at Raven.

While blocking the man's jump kick and rewarding him with an uppercut, Raven almost dislocated her wrist. She wasn't one to go down without putting up a fight. Blow after blow, the two opponents engaged in violent hand-to-hand combat. Judging from Jermaine's fighting style, he'd been trained in tae kwon do.

Jermaine's chin snapped back under her crescent kick, and Raven regretted the move as he tucked her in. *Wham!*

Raven, clotheslined with such cruelty, somersaulted onto her stomach. A warm sensation restricted the free movement of her hands, and her scalp cried for relief.

She'd become a hostage in Jermaine's deadly game. Raven expected to be the first to go, but he had other plans. He'd make her watch the others die in an attempt to instill fear coupled by guilt, taking the blame off himself. But who truly was to blame? Jermaine, who'd grown power hungry with each soul he possessed? Or the ones who sacrificed the men, women, and children to him?

"Ladies and gentleman," boasted Jermaine, armed with the shotgun. "This hunter, much like you, tried getting one over on me."

The Asian lady's jaws were prodded. A second later, her chair was covered in brain matter. She had been denied parting words and a final prayer.

"When you fuck with my money," Jermaine said as he laid another one to waste from behind, "you fuck with me."

Come on. Where the hell are you?

Raven watched Jermaine prance around and fire over his shoulder. "My mother told me to pick—"

"Hey, shit stain." Raven's lips squished together, and her cheeks pushed into her eyes.

"This white hooker got something to say?"

She kept silent.

"Didn't think so."

"Look left."

Bright headlights shone through bullet holes sprayed in the hangar doors. "What the—"

Daemoncles barged into the factory, and Jermaine fled for his life. With his arms outstretched, the bullets perforated Jermaine's torso, causing it to spout rivers of blood.

"I think we're even," said Daemoncles.

The laser cuffs short-circuited, and Raven headed for the last hostage. Those who'd been killed were expendable.

Daemoncles's crystal engine roared as though Satan himself had designed it. Its smoking guns scanned for more hostiles.

"You've gotta get me out of here," said Kevin.

"You sound like someone I know. Except he never made it home."

"Anything you want. Name it."

"I want a name."

"I don't understand," replied Kevin. Bifocals hung crookedly from his reddened face. He tipped over, and the bodies came with him.

"I find that odd for an insurance broker," said Raven.

She blew a ring of smoke and continued. "Fifty grand for each body. Two million for the shelter. I'm not believing you.

And if I ain't mistaken," Raven said as her cigarette butt sank into Jermaine's blood, "he didn't either."

The dead Asian's cold and abyssal eyes frowned upon Kevin.

"Thought she'd talk some sense into you."

"The bodies were just random immigrants. They'd bring 'em in, clean 'em up, and set 'em loose."

"Names!" Raven's harsh tone echoed, causing Kevin to piss his pants and choke up.

"They're everywhere. When the shelter came down, everybody got paid!"

Kevin's spectacles broke from a kick to the face, and a piece lodged into his eyelid.

"You insured these people, led them to a shelter, and profited from their deaths?" Her finger slid to the trigger.

The lunatic, bleeding from his iris, laughed and said, "And he enjoyed every minute of it."

The weapon's silencer slipped back.

"Thou sinners shall repent! Those who serve the devil will not enter the kingdom of—"

Kevin's head took the second set, shutting him up for good. He'd said what Raven feared to be true, and only one body was missing from the carnage.

———

"Who's that?" asked Enrico, pointing at the great golden statue inside the museum.

"Dominic Logan. The inventor of interdimensional travel."

The greatest mind who'd ever lived in the world posed with the drive to make the feat possible. Even so, no one was certain—except Logan himself—if it had worked at all. Raven made stops, like a tour guide, to answer every one of Enrico's questions. She had paid more attention in school than she remembered.

"What's that?"

"That's when people go far, far away into outer space."

"When's he coming back? I wanna go to outer space, too."

She hadn't the slightest clue. "Someday." She'd only seen the intimidating sculpture once as a child. And just like Enrico, Raven had been mesmerized beyond belief.

"And I'm sure he'll tell us all about it."

"When he does, you'll be an old man with stories of your own," said a familiar voice.

Raven turned to see Will dressed to impress and Deborah refusing to acknowledge Enrico's friendly wave.

"Quite a young lad you got there. Reminds me of myself when I was his age. Always seeking adventure."

"He wants to be a scientist one day."

"I do?"

She nudged her son, hoping he'd get the hint to play along.

"May I?" asked Will.

She was happy to oblige. "Go for it." She watched him lead Enrico to the Fish of Europa display. She and Deborah headed for the museum's dining room.

"No baby-sitter," snarled Deborah with a slight African accent and air of unchallenged certainty.

"No toothpaste?"

"Flea market?"

"No, but I see you've brought them."

Her fist would handle any further conversing.

Raven removed the name tag from her plate and speared a roll with her fork. Deborah sipped her wine and harrumphed at the same time.

A towering monolith was unveiled on center stage behind the podium. Raven guessed it was taller than any MechSoldier she'd faced in North Korea. WAR's banner hung high, and Mr. Sadiq Shamoon, WAR's CEO, entertained reporters and photographers.

"Tiffany, Tiffany, look what I got."

Raven felt the toy spaceship hit her bun and run over the top of it.

"A bit bold, I'd say. *Tiffany*? When I was a child..."

Will gave his wife a peck to shut her up and ordered a glass of Chardonnay.

Enrico undid his bow tie and picked out a piece of bread. He skipped the spoon and used the soup bowl instead.

"Enrico, watch your manners."

"Sorry, Mommy."

Raven smiled at his puffed cheeks chomping the hot morsel and downing a soda pop.

The who's who of Emerald Colony ordered endless entrées and beverages that were not easily affordable. Their plastic personas were ignorant of what people like her had been through. The majority didn't have a care in the world as they spent hundreds tipping the staff.

"My lady?"

Raven hadn't realized the waiter was there.

"We'll have beef and fries."

"And chicken nuggets," added Enrico.

Raven held back the tears as the table burst into laughter. Will didn't find anything amusing.

"Filet mignon? Steak, you mean? And potatoes?" clarified Will.

"Yeah…sounds appetizing."

"And broiled chicken for the little one—and more soup, please."

Deborah interrupted and said, "I'll have Europa squid."

How convenient, Raven thought. *The most expensive dish on the planet ordered by an expensive whore.*

"What is it you do for employment?" Deborah asked.

Given the opportunity, she'd show the wench. "Enrico's father is deployed to Italy." The boy's eye brows raised, and Raven covered his mouth before he could speak.

"A housewife?"

"You could call it that."

"And I will. You know, we could use an extra janitor around the studio if you're so inclined. Perhaps Enrico—"

Bishop Emmanuel's entrance saved Deborah's teeth from being knocked down her throat.

"Up," she whispered to Enrico.

The lights dimmed as the bishop led the guests in prayer. "Dear Heavenly Father, we thank you for the meal we are about to receive. Hear our prayers for those suffering outside our walls so they may find food and shelter. Let them find salvation through your son, Jesus Christ. Those who refuse to conform to the ways of Christ are the devil's children. And, I say, thou sinners shall repent. Those who serve the devil will not enter the kingdom of God. Amen."

"Amen," all but Raven repeated.

Enrico's eyes never left the podium, and Raven's hand squeezed, feeling a familiar tremble.

"Excuse us. We need to use the restroom."

Will offered no explanation and followed after.

"That's him," Raven told him.

"The bishop?" asked Will.

"I'm sure of it," replied Raven, holding Enrico's hand.

"You can't just go in there guns blazing."

"Watch me." She stopped in her tracks.

"Here. I'll get Enrico home. You take care of Emmanuel." Raven hesitated at first but handed over her son. "You're wasting time. Go."

———

"Colonists of Emerald, I present to you the Enforcer," said Mr. Shamoon, welcoming the applause.

The black curtain dropped, revealing a ten-foot monstrosity. Steel and advanced weaponry fused with genetically engineered flesh. The crowd hooted and hollered at the Qatari's work of pure genius. Or was it madness? The scientist responsible for the protective force field—and Goliaths incinerating citizens and soldiers alike—had amassed his vast fortune selling weapons of mass destruction.

Carlita rolled up her sleeves and used the watch to secretly access Sadiq's data pad.

"With your support, I can make Emerald Colony safe from homegrown and domestic terrorists alike."

Ironically, Sadiq himself was unofficially labeled an international terrorist.

"And with my creation, I can make a better future for your children."

Mr. Shamoon, in all his glory, initiated the Enforcer's start-up sequence. Or so he thought. Its center medallion glowed a darkish red, and it spoke. "Enforcer One online." Sadiq, awarded a standing ovation, was unable to finish reading the teleprompter.

Carlita witnessed Sadiq try to keep his cool as a fellow scientist whispered to him. Sadiq began to tread unfamiliar territory, having lost control and being forced to improvise.

Believing this was part of the show, one sloshed guest asked, "Can it do tricks?" His buddies high-fived him for having the courage to speak to Mr. Shamoon.

"I'll show you a trick." Carlita activated Enforcer1's weaponry, singled out herself, and watched the fireworks.

Screams of death and horror filled the dining room. Body upon body met a grim fate, shredded by the machine's lasers. The exits were jammed as the crowd struggled to escape; Enforcer1 cleared each fatal funnel.

Carlita unholstered the pistol underneath her red dress and said, "You're not getting away that easily." She shot two bodyguards and went after Sadiq, who'd escaped.

The brains of a trigger-happy security officer who had been protecting the launch pad doors were blown out. Carlita killed three human shields, released the mag, and reloaded.

"Target's trying to escape," a mercenary transmitted into her earpiece.

"He's not to leave. I want him alive," said Carlita into her watch.

Enforcer1 destroyed squads of ECPD SWAT officers who were attempting to evacuate the surviving colonists. Their armored vehicles and hovercrafts didn't stand a chance against the machine's high-tech weaponry.

Carlita's mercenaries engaged in a deadly firefight with Sadiq's men. Outnumbered and outgunned, their technology counted for nothing. Carlita emerged from the museum and mopped up the remnants of Sadiq's crew. His turban squished in Carlita's hand, and she dragged him to the edge of the roof.

Fire, smoke, fleeing colonists, and gun battles transformed Emerald Colony into a war zone.

"Take a look." Carlita pushed his head down. "Is this the future you had in mind?"

She stepped back between two mercenaries, pistol to her side and brown hair flowing in the wind. Sadiq was on his knees, arms raised in the belief that Allah would grant him mercy.

"The date chip—give it to me," ordered the Latina.

Sadiq continued in prayer, reciting the Koran. *Slap!*

"That was not a request. The data chip."

"*Allahu Akbar—*"

Thud!

"Now!" Carlita threw the turban over the edge and into a smoldering fire. Blood and spit dripped from Sadiq's beard. His eyes squinted at the laser from her pistol.

"I'll take it if I have to." Bombs and explosions rocked the airspace. Emerald's finest dwindled in numbers and succumbed to Joint Task Force Command. Fighters cracked the night sky, firing laser-guided missiles at its protective force field. The machine matched weapon for weapon and ate every infantryman and pilot alive.

"Slowly."

Sadiq removed the data pad from his clothing and entered the security code. The chip slid out a side compartment; once she had it, Carlita kicked Sadiq over and said, "Bring him."

A large black hovercraft touched down on the museum. Its bay doors opened, and they brought the scientist aboard.

"I hope you don't mind the sudden change of plans," she said. Carlita stashed the dress into a rack and fastened the two drop holsters to her cargo pants.

"What are you going to do to me?" he asked.

"That depends on you, Mr. Shamoon." A maneuvering fighter spun 180 degrees and disappeared into darkness that'd become the business district.

"Your war machines have killed thousands of my people and enslaved countless others," said Carlita. "My country is a sandbox, thanks to you and your…enterprise."

Mr. Shamoon was silent.

Smack!

"This ends now. You will give El Salvador back to my people, or yours will suffer."

"Maybe you ought to have a look in the mirror and ask yourself who is truly responsible!" cried Sadiq.

Carlita, insulted beyond reason, planted a kick into Sadiq's chest. Kneeling on his stomach, gun pointed at his head, she replied, "I've made kings squeal for mercy and turned entire civilizations against them. Soon you will see just how real I am."

———

Machines from WAR's Emerald-based factory answered Enforcer1's distress signal. Emerald Colony had made a deal with the devil. The banquet was only a prelude of what was to come. Thousands of Enforcers, armed for deployment, entered the battle for Emerald Colony.

Raven floored Daemoncles and burned rubber, turning corners and dodging missiles. No end scenario would stop her. A pastor shot Daemoncles from the bishop's sunroof. His body was dismembered as an Enforcer flew overhead. The driver cut a sharp left, and Daemoncles hydroplaned. Raven's steering wheel developed a mind of its own. She lost control of the vehicle and crashed into a car dealership.

"Shit! Shit! Shit!" exclaimed Raven.

The hiss from the tire added to her frustration. She had been so damn close. Raven kicked the deflated tire and yelped. She replaced her high heels with boots and salvaged weapons and ammo. She tossed and caught the vehicle's power chip and said, "Time for a new look."

Old habits refused to die. This time the police wouldn't pursue her on a fifteen-mile chase. Raven tore the sales tag off the luxury sedan, and, surprisingly, it was unlocked.

System Activated.

Highways, back roads, and all plausible ways out were flooded with colonists. They traveled by any means possible to escape the district's inner limits. Bombs and screaming rockets created fireballs, buildings were leveled, and its occupants were killed.

A hurricane had passed through the apartment's foyer and turned over vending machines and clothing articles. A dead man's head became sandwiched in the elevator.

She skipped each second step. Her body perspired profusely, and the blouse showed under her dress. A man and his family passed by at the eighth floor. Luggage in hand, the father said to Raven, "Didn't you hear?" Of course she had. "They're bringing in the big one."

And that was why Raven needed to find Enrico. She'd never be able to live with herself if something happened to him.

Apartment doors had been left wide open, the floor smelled of burned popcorn, and scavengers stole anything that wasn't nailed down.

"Enrico! Enrico!" No answer.

Welcome back, Tiffany...

"Shut up, Francis! Where's my son? Enrico!" No luck in his room, the bathroom was empty, and the study was how she had left it.

Since you and Enrico left this evening, no one's stopped by.

Raven felt cold, her heartbeat became rapid, and she couldn't speak. She checked under the bed and tore off the covers. The eruptions came closer. Raven walked in circles and teared up.

"We thought you'd come back here," said Will.

"Where is he?" Raven brought the RK72 up to her shoulder.

"He's safe."

"I will blow your fucking head off if you don't hand over my son!"

"Just take it easy."

"You hear that? No one will come looking for you."

"We took him to a safe location."

"Who's this 'we'?"

"I'll explain on the way. Just put the gun down."

"Explain this." The rifle fired blanks. Raven jumped at Will as he pulled a pistol and shot her.

The man she'd grown to trust, to whom she had confessed her darkest secrets and made love, betrayed her with a single bullet. The rifle slipped from her grasp, her feet crossed, and she fell, hitting her head on the nightstand. Captain Mallory's precognition was nothing short of a dark prophecy. All her drug-induced, irrational lifestyle choices had come back to bite her in the ass. At the gates of heaven only to be damned to hell. With each breath, possibly the last, Raven summoned every ounce of strength in her numbing body.

Let's get her up.

The exit's blocked.

What about the roof?
No good.
Shit. I told you to—
Hey! You gonna complain or—
Pop-pop!
Motherfucker! Can you believe it?
It's the end of the world.
Yeah, well, I'd rather die with a beer in my—
Be careful with her head.
Did you fuck her?
What?
Did you fuck her? I wanna know.
No.
Liar.
Nice shot.
Before ya know it, the whole world—
Cover us!
They're everywhere!
No shit!
This barrier's not gonna hold.
Ethan, hurry the fuck up!
There he is.
How's she doing?
Vitals are good.
Hold on!
Who taught you to fly?
Yo' momma!
She's gonna be pissed.
Yeah, well, I'll let you break the news.

Fuck, man.
I know how you feel.
Whole damn colony's gone.
Control, we're coming in hot!
Seven percent damage.
Copy that!
Whew!
Thank God.
That was close.
Watch her head.

The *Virginia*

Location Unknown—December 2, 2172

SHE PUT TWO hands on her stomach and vomited the clear liquid used to sustain nutrition levels. The unpalatable aftertaste of black licorice rested on her tongue. Raven used the thick blanket to cover herself and took in her surroundings. A floating bioscanner showed an x-ray of her unbearably aching body, plagued with the buildup of lactic acid. The hot sensation of Will's tranquilizer coursing through her veins was all she could remember before blacking out.

Chatter and an occasional laugh passed outside the door. Nameless shadows followed footsteps, hurrying up and down the hall to attend pressing matters.

Amazingly, the floor felt warm on her single bare foot. The other came down on top of the smooth marble surface, and she unscrewed the intravenous needle from its tube. Raven couldn't fathom what she was seeing. Her inner being felt this outstanding sense that it had been disembodied from an empty shell. Immortalized in this afterlife. Free from the physical limitations imposed by a three-dimensional existence. This universe was different. It was at peace with itself and continued to grow, expanding beyond the reaches of humanity and its biased understanding of all things living, dead, or yet to come.

A ten-fingered imprint stained the window to her new world. Outside the glass, a set of large bay doors opened to a smaller spacecraft that touched down on a blue-beaconed launchpad.

"Raven?" The infirmary's doors hadn't made a sound, allowing Will to enter unnoticed. "How are you feeling?"

"What...is this? Where am I?" Her throat was parched, and her lips were dry.

"I'm glad to see you're up," he said, responding without answering.

"Where's Enrico? Why does everything hurt so much?"

"One thing at a time." Will guided Raven to the bed and filled a glass of water. The cool liquid brought relief to her desiccated throat. She gulped the water to the last drop, as though her life depended on it. And it did, judging by the state of dehydration she felt.

"We got Enrico out just in time; he's safe on deck."

"I'm confused." She was finally able to speak without stuttering.

"He didn't put up any fuss. He was tranquilized as well, to lessen the shock."

"I'll ask again. Where am I?"

"Tiffany, let me be the first to welcome you aboard the *Virginia*." None of it made a bit of sense. And neither did he.

"Tiffany!"

"Enrico!" She gave the little one a hearty hug and kissed his forehead. Enrico smiled and pretended to shoot the spacecraft descending into the *Virginia*. Well, he was getting his wish—perhaps a lot sooner than she'd expected.

"It's going to take some time before you're fully adjusted, and it's been a few days since you've eaten."

Raven was too dumbfounded to recognize her stomach tried to eat itself. A nurse laid down a set of bath towels and a bottle of soap.

"The nurse will see to it you're cleaned up. After a hot shower, why don't you join us for dinner?"

After a relaxing hot bath in the ship's bathroom, Raven was escorted to join Will, Deborah, and Enrico for a mouth-watering meal of fried chicken, greens, and biscuits in the dining area. The ship's cooks prepared a special request, baking a handful of nuggets.

"Much better than what the museum was serving, wouldn't you say, Enrico?" said Will, giving him a smile.

Will started pouring Raven a drink of Scotch. She waited till the glass reached shot level, gulped it, and slammed it down. She closed the cigarette lighter and addressed Enrico. "Get up. We're leaving."

"Hold it, Raven. There are some things we needed to talk about, but it's best you settle in first," said Will. "Get some food in you. A good night's rest—"

"You lie to me, kidnap me and my son, and then pretend I can just adjust to being hauled halfway to wherever the hell this is. Thank you, but fuck you." She took Enrico's hand and said, "Let's go."

"Kidnap, you say? If I'm not mistaken, that boy is not your property either," snarled Deborah.

Punch!

Blood gushed from the bitch's nose; Will rushed over with a handkerchief.

The writing aboard the craft was alien in nature, so Raven used the shuttle bay outside the window for guidance. A passing soldier in armor witnessed Deborah and Will exit the dining area and then looked at Raven. She kicked the soldier in the gut and yanked his weapon from its holster.

"Back up," she demanded, pointing the soldier's own weapon at his head.

"Let her go," ordered Will.

"Where we going?" asked Enrico, quickly following.

"Home."

The corridor ended at a locked door, and Raven aimed the weapon at its control panel. "Stand back."

Before the pistol could fire, however, she clutched her stomach and curled into a fetal position.

"Raven!" cried Enrico.

"What's happening to me?" said Raven, shuddering.

Enrico's voice trailed off, and she saw two soldiers grabbing at him. The pistol wobbled and slipped from her hand.

The darkness returned. She felt the stinging liquid from an injection and yanked at the nurse's hair. "What have you done to me?" Those were her last words before it was over.

———

She caressed his hair and kissed him good night. His hair smelled like vanilla soap and was soft to the touch. Raven fled her quarters hours after coming to, and, ironically, the soldier she had attacked showed her to Enrico's room. She apologized on the way down, and he accepted. *Maybe I'm overreacting*—a passing thought she immediately cast aside. No one—and she meant *no one*—was getting close to her or Enrico.

The boy turned in his sleep at the sound of a rising door.

"Raven," said Will.

She eyed the intimidating militaristic blues, high-glossed shoes, and white sash across his chest.

"Come with me," said Will.

"I don't know who or what you are, but you take us home."

"You wanted answers. You'll get answers. Now, please follow me."

She watched him dismiss two soldiers serving as bodyguards. "Don't take it personally. The serum hasn't completely worn off."

After traversing numerous corridors and passageways, they came to a double door guarded by a set of soldiers. Will gave a sharp salute, and what Raven saw next took her breath away.

"Welcome to the *Virginia*'s operation center."

A spectacular view of the stars served as the backdrop for busy workers tending to motherboards and various computers. A heavily equipped man, unlike the soldiers she'd seen, brushed by Raven on his way out, but she continued to stare. Holographic monitors displayed the war in Emerald Colony and firefights between armored soldiers and Enforcers. She noticed the soldiers were wearing the same getup as the one who'd just left.

"This is where we keep track of all hunter operations on Earth," said Will, maximizing one of the monitors.

Will had promised answers, but this was far too much. No wonder he had waited till her head cleared. "Hunters?" she asked, holding her temple.

"This way, if you will."

Raven followed him to another room she guessed was his personal office. After the door closed, she took a much-needed seat. Her eyes shot toward a bottle of bourbon on the wall, so he fetched a glass and poured her a shot.

"Aren't you glad I waited?"

"This is—"

"I know—a lot," he finished. Joining her, he took a sip and refilled her glass. "The *Virginia* is attached to what's known as the Intergalactic Sol Federation."

"You've lost me already."

Raven moved her arms back, watching Will's desk light up. A beautiful blue planet resembling Earth floated in the center, although it appeared to be much larger in mass.

"Eve. Humanity's second home. I don't want to bore you with a history lesson. You'll find all you need to know on your new Oplink."

Will swiped the hologram aside using his palm. He leaned on the desk and said, "I'll cut to the chase, Raven. Aaron approaching you after the war ended was no coincidence."

She remembered now. The guy who'd left a calling card on her when she was passed out in a back alley. He had claimed to be a part of some secret squirrel agency hiring vets. The income wasn't stable, but it was too good a deal to turn down.

"We've had you on our radar for a very long time now. Your ability to do what is necessary to get the job done is what I'm looking for." He coughed at the ring of smoke hitting his face.

"That's great to know. Why am I here?"

Will gave her the answer in the form of hologram showing a burning colony.

"What you're witnessing is the work of a rogue hunter—a wanted fugitive whose crimes have called for her execution."

She didn't have to ask what this all meant. Her gaze attached to the fire engulfing Emerald Colony.

A shooting star behind Will grabbed her attention. Part of her wished it would take her away. The other part wished she were dreaming. She'd wake up, grab a burger and a beer, and start the day. Wishful thinking.

"Hunters such as you are a rare breed. And every so often we come to Earth to seek out the very best. My crew is full of men and women trained since birth. It's all they've ever known. They lack the natural human instinct to make a decision without relying on what they've been fed at the academy—or to do what is right even when they know it's wrong."

The picture of a middle-aged Latina took the burning hologram's spot. Assassination, theft, murder, conspiracy to commit terrorism—the list went on.

"The woman before you is Carlita Lopez. We have every reason to believe she was behind the terrorist attack in Emerald Colony."

Raven crossed one leg over the other, took a drink, and asked, "If she's so hot, why don't you go after her? Don't take that personally."

"And that is why I need your help."

Raven took another hit of bourbon. A lunatic to catch a lunatic. Who would've guessed?

"I need someone who is able to think on her toes. Someone who can think—I'm afraid to say—as a human. Carlita is much like you. An Earth native recruited decades ago to join the federation. She has a grudge against WAR for the atrocities committed in El Salvador."

"What's in it for me?"

"The opportunity of a lifetime—the chance to join the ISF and see things you'd never dreamed possible."

Was he lying? Possibly. She'd had her suspicions, and he'd lied before. But lately, protecting and giving Enrico a new home had become more of a priority than her own selfish indulgences. She'd never imagined it'd be light-years away on some alien planet. "If I don't make it back..."

"He'll be well taken care of. Trust me."

"Thanks."

"You'll be supplied with customized gear and weapons for the mission. Things have gone to shit, and Raul's declared martial law across all four colonies. I'd hate for you to get caught short."

"So he's running the show?"

"By constitutional law, the senior governor is placed in charge during a national emergency. Whatever you do, do not interfere." His words were very cold.

The butt of Raven's cigarette sizzled in the tray, and she stood up.

"Training begins first thing tomorrow," said Will.

———

"We'll start whenever you're ready," said the training official, Sam, showing his pudgy face in the Oplink's hologram.

Raven listened and waited for the Oplink to connect to the ISF2100. The Oplink was her new lifeline—far more efficient and reliable than the watch she'd grown accustomed to. Weapons and armor integration, global positioning, and worldwide data and research capabilities were a few of the features linked to the system. She kept the old code name for some familiarity.

A double yank of the gauntlets, a pat on the chest armor, a drop of the visor, and she was ready for action.

"Let's do this."

The next thing she knew, she was harnessed inside a strange spacecraft in what looked like the *Virginia*'s shuttle bay.

Hold on to your seats, ladies and gentlemen, transmitted Sam.

Raven strained her neck and witnessed the lights flashing rapidly, jetting out past the bay doors. The roar of the engines became louder; her Kevlar and hands vibrated slightly, and she held on to her harness. She listened to a monstrous metallic sound over the main engine, noticing the bay doors were starting to lift.

Prepare for lift-off in three…two…one.

Raven's body shot sideways at lightning speed, her vision twisting 180 degrees and then coming full circle. The helmet's

HUD dropped in target elevation and range. Within minutes, which seemed like seconds, the nose of the shuttle deflected flame as it began its descent into Earth's atmosphere.

The drop point's too hot. Setting new coordinates.

Blue turned to a dark and bleak gray; the windows iced with rain, and the craft broke left.

Flashes of red shot past the window, forcing the craft to conduct evasive maneuvers.

The back end of the craft burst into flames and then ripped apart. Weapon racks and equipment dropped into the darkened clouds.

Raven used the thermal imager to navigate through the black fumes and released the seat's harness—a terrible mistake. Her armor sustained the brunt of the hit as the pilot's console burst and—*BAM!*

With her rifle locked on to the back plate of her armor, she gathered every ounce of strength and bashed the seat from her path. The bolts on the second row rattled; this time she wouldn't be as fortunate.

Alternating hand and boot, blocking falling debris, and struggling to keep from sliding down, Raven crawled to the rear. The shuttle was in an uncontrolled glide, but it wouldn't last much longer. Soon it would take a nose dive, destroying the shuttle and killing her in the process.

Raven, your armor is equipped with emergency boosters. You'll be able to access them through the Oplink.

The remaining row of seats helped balanced her weight. Cycling through the hologram, she located the suit's booster function and initiated the countdown sequence—thirty seconds.

You're right over the drop point. You won't get a second chance. Go!

The moment Raven's feet left the deck, the craft descended on a crash course into Emerald Colony. Thousands of years in advanced technology would be scattered across the earth—free game to whoever recovered it. If the JTF got their hands on it first and reversed engineered it, only God knew what would come next.

The armor emitted a steady tone, and after switching from blue to white, the two light panels raised, skyrocketing Raven head first toward Emerald.

Zooming in, the insertion point's range lowered, countless lasers and rockets exchanged from end to end, a lucky few igniting their intended targets. Calling Emerald Colony a war zone was an understatement. Korea was a war zone. This was World War III—machine versus man. And from the looks of it, there'd be no winners. The entire species annihilated with the push of a button.

A large explosion occurred in the easternmost part of the district—the craft coming to rest.

Raven, you're coming in too fast. You've got a Goliath twelve hundred meters from the IP.

An array of charred skeletons and dismembered corpses held a welcoming party as Raven closed in. Feet first, boosters retracting, Raven retrieved the ISF2100 and prepped for a hard landing.

Two extremities of the eight-legged machine locked onto Raven and fired just as she hit the ground and rolled to cover. She kept her torso to the wall as the laser peeled the bricks away.

A steady blast of firepower shattered the cockpit window, shredding the operator. Blood and guts seeped out the sides. The machine buckled, and the weight of its fall sent an aftershock her way.

Prepare to copy.

"Send it."

The ship you were riding in crashed approximately five hundred meters from where you're standing. I need you to hightail to the shuttle and destroy its drive system.

"Copy that."

Some order this was. Upon impact, every available body was closing in on its location. She'd have to play it smart to complete the order. *We cannot let anyone get their hands on that technology.*

Raven set her sights on a nearby shop. The remaining glass of the shop broke apart from the force of a steel fist. Had the suit been any thicker, she'd be stuck in the window, ass end out.

The temperature gauge in the HUD read a blistering five degrees Fahrenheit. Weaver ready to kill on sight, Raven trotted through the rubble, cracking empty bottles and supplies under her steel boots. The storage had been picked clean of resources by panicked colonists. Survival instinct had taken precedence over materialistic desire—the main safe was still intact. How far they'd made it was anyone's guess.

An adult male and a small child lay dead in the grocery aisle. Wielding a crowbar, the male had died defending his son. A closer look and she'd notice this was the father from the stairwell. There'd been four at the time, but now the wife and daughter were missing. This wasn't the work of a machine but a gang of sex-starved lunatics, taking advantage of the chaos to commit the darkest of crimes.

She kicked out an exit door and scanned left and then right. At full speed, the shoulder pads collided with the door, sending it crashing down. The sounds of a violent gun battle bounced from wall to wall in the restaurant. The Enforcer was bent over backward, its lifeless eyes stared back. *Dead?* It had never been alive to begin with. Her weapon's barrel tapped the medallion, producing a clinking noise. Its steel had been charred from a blast or high-powered weapon. The center medallion's protective shield was split apart and instead of a red glow, the piece was a blunt, darkish brown.

What are you? She thought, disgusted, looking at the half man, half machine.

Dismembered corpses and scraps of metal littered the alley ahead. Across the way was a side door leading into the Nefertiti.

Explosive rounds selected.

A miniature blue disk spiraled out of the rifle.

Boom! The entrance combusted and crumbled in a blackish smoke.

What's your status?

"I'm headed up now."

There's armor en route in that direction, but they're taking a lot of resistance. It'll buy you some time, but you need to hurry.

"I'm on it," she transmitted, simultaneously holstering and unholstering weapons.

"Shit." The elderly man toppled, and Raven pushed the bullet-riddled wheelchair from the elevator. It was suicide, but she would die from exhaustion scaling eighty floors' worth of steps. The elevator was still in working condition, and the ascent was smooth until...

No need to panic. Two clicks—no good. A third—still nothing. Back against the wall, the elevator swayed, and a she heard a loud screeching noise. Somewhere between the seventy-sixth and seventy-ninth floor, she hung on the edge of plummeting to her death.

The Nefertiti's engineers had chosen luxury over safety, and she was paying for it. But the decision did have an advantage she was sure they'd taken into account. With two rounds placed into the corners of the upper portion, the small maintenance hatch hung briefly before twisting off. The armor's weight didn't make her particularly agile. Raven's first attempt ended on the floor, causing additional damage to the elevator's suspension system. Straining and grunting, she gave it all she had. One leg after the other, she made it into the shaft. The celebration was short-lived because within seconds, the suspension system gave way. In one miraculous leap, her feet were dangling as she watched the elevator drop at a tremendous speed.

Boom!

Shocked from nearly dying, Raven held on tight until the tremors ceased before moving on.

What was that? Are you OK?

"I'm taking the scenic route."

They've closed in on the shuttle. Double-time it.

Raven emerged on the eightieth floor bruised but still functioning. She raced in the direction of an exit sign, only to be stopped in her tracks.

There it was again. The scream. Tortured howls far from where anyone besides Raven could hear them—or care.

"*No, please stop. Aggh!*"

Through the exit, and, like a trained marksman's, each bullet found its target—two to the chest and one to the head. The second one hit the assailant in the back while he was trying to escape.

She found the man's other half. Beaten, battered, and bleeding from every orifice. As for his daughter...

Covered in unimaginable filth, the short-haired blonde looked upon Raven as if she'd been saved by death itself. The rain pelted off the armor, dripping down an amazing work of technological innovation. The Kevlar zapped and transformed to match the urban environment. Unapologetic, Raven pushed the woman from her path.

"I'm here," Raven transmitted. The fronts of the tanks were engraved with a JTF insignia and abbreviated markings. A second scan revealed a heat signature coming from the bed of a heavily guarded truck.

Target locked...guided grenade selected...fire when ready.

As Raven squeezed the trigger, the woman pushed her rifle, forcing her shot off target. A hundred meters away, it killed two soldiers providing perimeter security.

Steel connected with flesh, the woman's head bounced off a rail, and she came down on all fours.

"What the hell is wrong with you?" Her mouth dribbled a string of blood "They're the good guys," said the woman.

The truck was pulling out of range. A congregation of soldiers and armor began spreading out to find the source of the explosion. The search was amiss in the fog of war. She had only one chance to make it count. A line of crystal fuel tanks ran adjacent to the roadway.

Incendiary round selected.

Boom! Boom! Boom! Boom!

A violent chain reaction sent the truck up in a crimson inferno.

The barrel wavered, and it was pointing more at the ground than where the woman intended. "You killed them."

Barefooted, unclothed, eyes red, she footed backward, not wanting a full frontal confrontation. Icy breath blowing through chattering teeth, she tripped over the body but managed to maintain control of the weapon.

Daring her to fire, Raven clanked toward the fallen woman, who now was shaking more due to fright than the icy winds. Raven stripped the pistol from the woman's hands and flung it to the side.

Stand by for identification...

Zoe Pinfield, a twenty-eight-year-old biochemist employed by the Joint Space Agency. Other than a few traffic infractions, she was clean as a whistle.

Training scenario terminated.

Raven's heart was racing, and her body was soaked. The last thing she remembered was smacking a blonde who'd grabbed her weapon.

"Impressive, huh?" said Sam, entering from a hidden door. The older gentleman walked with a hobble and breathed heavily. His glasses had trouble staying on his face. "Outstanding work."

"How did you...what happened?"

"Environmental manipulation. We can accurately judge how a hunter will react in the field. What you've just experienced is one of a thousand possible scenarios when you return to Earth. It's the ones we can't foresee that worry us. I laughed when you socked that lady right in the kisser."

She didn't find a damn thing funny. All this time she'd believed it was real. At this moment she questioned if what she was feeling now was real. This kind of technology was dangerous in the wrong hands.

———

The four-eyed creature reminded Raven of a salamander she'd stepped on. Its one fang snapped, and it appeared to be chasing its long tail. A young red-haired girl patted the creature on the head and said to Enrico, "That's Juju." Enrico's eyes became large, and he brought his hands back. "Don't worry; he doesn't bite. When we go home, you'll get to meet him."

Raven associated the girl's paleness with lack of true sunlight. The pad collapsed, and a young boy from afar called over, "Chelsea! Mrs. Hardatt's taking us to the moon! She said to bring Enrico!"

"Can I go, please? Please?" Enrico asked.

The girl never left his side and pleaded as well. "Oh, please, Mrs. Raven. Can Enrico go? He says he's never been to the moon."

A trip to the moon? Are they insane? The only things to see were Lunar Crystal mining stations and the remnants of a failed time-travel experiment. Anyway, Enrico needed to make friends if she planned to stay. Keeping him locked up would only isolate him. He was no different from the others, and they needed to see that. Raven shook her head but said, "Go ahead."

"Thanks, Mrs. Raven. Wait for us!" yelled the little girl, running across the courtyard.

She held a blade of grass and squinted at the artificial sun placed in a lower-than-usual blue sky.

A group of teens were smoking near a bench, and a long-haired girl sat on the alpha male's lap. It never occurred to her how she was able to communicate with the crew until now. She'd ask Will later—speaking of the devil.

"Beautiful day, isn't it?" he said, sneaking up behind her.

"But is any of it real?" she replied, watching an eagle take flight.

"Technologically speaking…yes."

Not what she was looking for, but it would do.

"We have the Kri to thank for our species' survival. All you've seen is due to their generosity."

She recalled the Kri from glancing over Eve's file. What she didn't recall was reading it in the Bible shoved down her throat or any distorted book on ancient history. A male and female from every race transported over vast distances to begin a new world. Racial segregation and poverty were unspeakable to Eve's citizens. They lived in harmony with one another. No monetary system, homelessness, or starvation. Raven believed she'd never fit in. Living off others' scraps was the only way she'd ever lived.

"Tiffany?"

He asked, a second time, "Tiffany. Is everything all right?"

Now it was time for the real questions. She didn't care about the sun built in the middle of a spaceship. Or how she had fallen from the sky while standing still. It was time for the truth.

"Why'd you lie to me?" They stopped at a pond, and a fish sank under, leaving ripples over her reflection. "I want the truth."

"I was embedded in WAR to see the completion of a classified project. Aaron sent me status updates on your assignments, and honestly...I had to see for myself."

"So you moved in two doors down from me. It would've been a lot easier if you'd just asked."

"Not with the state you were in," replied Will.

Sure, she was an emotional mess and probably would've laughed in Will's face had he been truthful. He was right. It had to happen this way. Raven felt the arrow in her heart. It was too good to be true. A drunken one-night stand after happy hour had led to multiple nights sneaking out to do it all over again. All the promises about leaving his wife had been a lie. And there, staring at Will's quarters, was the cunt she'd grown to despise. She gave her the evil eye before abruptly closing the drapes. Will took notice and said, "I'd better get back." It was obvious who wore the pants between the two.

"Colonel," said a black lieutenant. "Sir, I think you need to see this."

She followed Will through the courtyard into sector one. Her sweat chilled against the corridor's air conditioner. They passed the VOC up to the *Virginia*'s flight deck. She feared the craft Enrico was in might've crashed, but her fears subsided when Will asked, "Did we lose a ship?" and the crew member replied, "Negative, sir."

The main communications console was surrounded by three other members listening to an inaudible transmission.

"Where's it coming from?" asked Will, looking at his lieutenant for an answer.

"We were able to triangulate the signal, and this is what we got," he replied, typing into the console. A dark-red planet and pieces of its moon loosely in orbit energized inside a holograph.

"Titus," said Will, never taking his eyes off the planet, "any idea who sent the distress call?"

Raven saw beads of perspiration on the lieutenant's forehead when he addressed Will, "No, sir. Soon as we got a lock, it just…disappeared."

"Send up the file. See if command can make anything of it."

"Roger that, sir."

This was all new to Raven, but seeing the crew's reaction and the sinister red of the planet's surface told her there was more to what had happened. The signal was not a mistake—it was a warning.

———

She didn't prolong her good-bye. Her words where short and sweet. She'd foregone any details and promised to return before long. She'd be gone before he awoke.

Raven choked up, but no tears were shed. She needed to be strong. For the two of them. If the simulations she'd undergone where any indication, she was in for one hell of a ride.

Corporal Tiffany Raven, Blood Type—O positive, 03/02/47, SN 053100, Spiritual Satanist. The dog tag hung loose over a green tank top, and her head hit the pillow. She tucked an arm underneath and let her mind travel beyond the stars. Raven's eyes chased a celestial body as it crossed the glass ceiling. Propped up on her elbows, she raised her eyebrows as she saw the anomaly change course. A magnificent blue light blasted it into infinity. She'd never envisioned seeing this sort of thing. What was it? Her heart repetitions accelerated at the thought of having witnessed an extraterrestrial intelligence. At this moment she knew there was no going back.

"The Plybb."

Will had a way of coming in unannounced. She sat up, and her feet dangled from the bed. She noticed the ringed planetary sphere embroidered on his blue sweat suit, and he'd recently showered. It was her favorite body wash of his. He stopped halfway to the bed, and Raven quickly ran into his arms.

The two lovers kissed and embraced each other in heated passion. The bulge between her fingertips had her body wanting it.

So hard and so thick. I need all of you, she told herself.

Raven's tank top stretched above her head, and she moaned, feeling Will suck her breasts. Her arms circled Will's sleek bald head, guiding him to their love nest. Shoes, pants, undies were tossed aside. Naked and unhampered, Will and Raven became one.

"Ugh." She was wet as ever. Slow, hard, and deep inside. "Ugh...Ugh." Feelings of fervor raced from head to toe. She wanted this to last forever—making love beneath an endless sea of stars. Will's tongue penetrated Raven's mouth, and she rolled him over to be on top.

She eased her rhythm to stop Will from cumming. Her body moistened, and she pulled out. Down to his pelvis, she wasted no time tonguing and licking Will's tasty nut sack. She gauged and matched his movements to her caresses.

A flavorsome treat of precum oozed from Will's cock. Raven licked up every bit of it before swallowing his shaft. Not too fast or too slow. She sucked Will's black dick nice and even to make it last. No hands—just her mouth. Swarms of delectation filled her mouth and body.

She was aching for another fucking. Raven popped the cock out her mouth and moved to cowgirl.

Breasts and abs glistening, hair dropped from its bun, Raven fucked Will as fast as she could. The bed rocked, and she didn't give a damn whose ears were pressed against her wall. Her pussy tightened, and her nipples became hard. She came and tickled Will's balls at the same time. He followed suit and cream-pied Raven's hot pussy.

Hair wild, bodies steaming, the aroma of hot sex circulating the room, she felt him soften but wanted more. More of Will's sexy body and hard cock. To the naked eye, Raven looked like an untamed cavewoman whose hunger for sex was insatiable. She listened to Will's heavy breathing as her ass pushed up on his stomach.

The dim fluorescent lighting from the corridor of the crew quarters was visible once more. The mysterious shadow outside her door had moved on. Raven deviously smiled and licked her succulent lips.

Hunter-Prey

RIFLE IN HAND, side arm attached to her leg, fully geared for war, boots clanking against the bay's metal grates. This was the first time she'd returned since arriving days ago. Maintenance men and women worked feverishly repairing shuttles. A small group took their lunch break near a craft they'd been repairing. Hands black as night, they chomped on sandwiches and sipped beers.

Drinking on the job. My kind of people.

As directed, she rode the elevator to the lower launch level. She then walked toward the flashing lights beneath a fired-up craft. To her left was an unobstructed view of space. Realistically speaking, the vacuum should've swiped her up, but the monster-sized bay door was constructed using an unseen material. Just one of the many things that continued to fascinate her.

By the shuttle's hatch were Will and an Asian male she'd never met before. Not much of a farewell party.

Will's eyes turned from Raven. No "good morning" or "thanks for letting me sneak into your room last night." Oh well. She had gotten what she'd wanted.

Will finally looked up and said, "Raven, I'd like you to meet Kichiro. He'll be your point of contact while you're in the field."

Raven nodded at Kichiro, who said, "Glad to be at your service." The teen was young enough to be Enrico's big brother.

Will continued. "Everything from extraction requests to supply drops will go through Kichiro. He'll keep me abreast of your status. Raven, please keep in mind that this mission is strictly classified."

She locked the rifle into the rack and asked, "So I'm going in alone?"

"I'm afraid so. Very few are privileged to the mission's details. Your communication with Kichiro is on a frequency undetectable by the VOC. I can't afford to take the risk."

"Where's my IP?"

Will motioned and said, "Kichiro."

"Carlita's gone dark, but her prisoner bar code is virtually untraceable. Ironically, Aaron's new recruit did a bit of home-work and traced Sadiq to Emerald Prison. Unfortunately, the recruit was killed during the investigation."

"She's running interference."

"Correct," replied Will to Raven's intuitiveness. "We believe she's using a cloaking device. Prisoner bar codes are irremovable. She'd kill herself in the process."

"What about Sadiq?"

Will said the unexpected. "Sadiq's a second priority. If he's not dead already, see to it he makes it out alive."

Two well-known terrorists capable of inconceivable horrors given a slap on the wrist. Raven kept her opinions on Sadiq to herself. She was only to follow orders. "Well...what are we waiting for?"

"Good luck." With no final kiss to send her off, Will turned away. Pressure released from the hatch, and Will and Kichiro headed down the ramp. Butterflies filled her stomach as she heard the locks secure. This was no training scenario. This was as real as the hairs standing on her neck. Raven's head was enclosed in a sleek black visor helmet, and she connected the Oplink.

The engine ignited a steady hum, and she strapped in.

All systems online and ready for launch, transmitted Kichiro through Raven's HUD. *Prepare for lift-off in three...two...*

Boom!

Without any abrupt twist and turns, the acceleration was much smoother than the simulation.

Stars zipped past the pilotless craft, and shortly a breathtaking view of the Earth appeared. Vast blue oceans, never-ending green landscapes. So big, yet so insignificant in the grand scale of things.

Raven, you're not going to like this.

"Try me."

I'm detecting what looks like a rebel faction closing in on the prison. My guess is they've been tipped off. Everyone wants a piece of this guy.

"A civil war."

My thoughts exactly. Fight your way inside and get Sadiq the hell out of there.

Smoke from burning buildings, Enforcers trampling the streets, angry colonists turned scared or detained for protesting. Emerald Colony resembled Korea at its worst in only a week's time. WAR had regained control of its arsenal, but what price did Emerald's colonists have to pay for a dawning Orwellian future? There was only one answer: blood.

Raven, you're approaching the IP. Prepare for deployment.

The hatch released, and Raven was welcomed by a sun straining through an overcast sky. Cold and unforgiving, the wind gusted against the armor, but it wasn't enough to stop a war heroine.

The suit's rear thrusters engaged, and Raven descended upon Emerald Colony. Burst of small-arms fire were seen in the abandoned courtyard between Carlita's hired guns and rebel factions. She aimed her body at a nearby manned guard tower and prepped for landing.

Into a murky body of water, her boots splashed up thick globs of filth.

A running head shot, and the man in the tower dropped lifeless.

Bang! Bang! Bang! Bang! Bang! Bang!

She let the factions murder one another while scoping for an entrance. A side door fifty meters away from the tower was her first option. Out the door filed three Latinos hoping to get a jump on the rebels. Raven's ISF2100 ended their plans.

A silent enemy locator fired from Raven's weapon and attached itself inside the door. Her HUD transmitted a live feed—one tango armed and kneeling to the right of the entrance.

Pop! He never saw her coming.

Dark, musty, and dank. The abandoned prison was growing mold, and specks of daylight shone through cracked windows. On the floor were loose papers and broken furniture. A tremendous explosion rocked the prison walls, destroying pieces of the crumbling ceiling. A blasting machine gun returned fire.

Raven, I'm going to connect into your Oplink and widen the locator's range.

Raven took cover inside an old office and timed her shots. As the voices broke the threshold, she reappeared in the hallway and shredded four men alive.

"Hurry up, damn it. They know I'm here."

Got it. There's a heavy concentration near solitary confinement.

"They've fallen back to protect the package. I'm going in." Numerous specks of red filled Raven's HUD. A lone individual was isolated from the pack. She turned the character blue to avoid terminating her target.

Hurry, Raven. The rebels have breached the perimeter.

The main holding cells had a striking resemblance to an old horror movie. Empty human cages vandalized in graffiti by violent gang members and thugs. Raven turned her eyes at the rotting corpse—a homeless colonist killed while asleep.

They were using an all-too-familiar defense tactic. Raven armed a flash grenade and kicked in the door. The visor darkened, and time slowed to a crawl.

The first victim's head exploded, and the next took one to the chest. A body was riddled from the burst of her weapon, and the one next to him was sprayed to join the others in death.

Uncontrolled shots hit the ceiling as more men fell victim. The floor and cell doors were painted into a portrait of blood and guts. A dying body pleading for mercy was put out of his misery.

Raven looked at the frail and beaten Muslim curled in the corner. The door's security system was short-circuited from a bullet.

"Stand up. I'm here to get you out."

The timid Qatari's hands shook, and he replied, "Leave me be."

"I don't have time for this shit. I said"—Sadiq's dirty hair entangled into Raven's gauntlet—"stand up!" And then, to Kichiro, she transmitted, "Target's secured. I need an exit."

Searching...searching...got it. Check your HUD.

"Don't move!" yelled a rebel. His six was quickly surrounded with more of his ilk. She saw his head and eyes move up and down.

"You've done us a great service, soldier. Now hand him over, and we'll consider letting you walk out of here alive."

Sweat was streaming down her armpits; the weapon was heavy.

"Get behind me," she said through clinched teeth.

"That muthafucka gonna pay for what he's done. Hand him over!"

More weapons charged, and lasers dotted the armor.

"Things are going to get really hot. Whatever you do, don't move."

"People died 'cause of his sorry ass. And you wanna protect dis sand nigga?"

Raven used her eye contacts to access the Oplink, and moments later a red circle burned into the floor. A hole gave way, and the rebels fired.

Slam! Thud!

"Move!" she ordered Sadiq.

Bullets rained from above, narrowly missing them both.

"We gotta go, man! They after us!" called out a rebel. They gave the drop a second thought and retreated.

Screams of death and bloodshed rang outside the walls. Raven felt an unmistakable trotting vibration and listened to chained artillery annihilate the rebels.

"The woman who kidnapped you—where is she?"

"She escaped with everything—" he said, coughing. "Access codes, data files, prototypes. She left her men to die."

Raven knew it wouldn't be long before WAR sent out a search party. And Carlita had bailed just as the fireworks were starting.

Sadiq held his ankle and said, "She's planning to shut down the system." He coughed loudly. "She must be stopped. It'll ruin everything I've worked for."

A cease-fire silenced the fog of war. The rebels were crushed, and none had survived the onslaught.

"Can you walk?"

"I believe so."

Through the damp basement, they came to an exit door. She kicked it open; the area was clear of rebel forces. Sadiq took advantage of his newfound freedom and fled the prison.

"Sadiq, wait," called out Raven.

"Praise Allah," cried Sadiq, his arms held high at the circling rotorless helicopter.

She took up a position behind a cruddy window and watched the warmonger kneel and kiss the ground, praying to his god.

The window vibrated, and she pulled back out of sight, weapon at the ready for the unexpected. Her mouth was shut, and her ears were open.

The Enforcer's chain gun started to rotate.

"No. No. What are you doing?"

A hell-spawned blast of lasers tore Sadiq's body into pieces.

"Sadiq was just assassinated," transmitted Raven.

I'm not sure whether that's a bad thing or good thing.

"If Carlita's aiming for WAR's central AI system, she'll shut down the entire planet."

We can't let that happen. I think I've located the device she's using to mask her movements.

"Send it."

You need to head under Emerald's subway system. Since this whole thing kicked off, the system's been offline. Sending a decryption code to you now.

"Got it." Raven maximized the six-digit code for a better reading.

The device is black marketed. Mostly used by escape convicts from Plybberia. Somehow she's been able to increase its power to cover the whole colony. Decrypt the device, and she'll have nowhere to hide.

Caged

THE WOMAN'S RAGS were soaked, and her stomach was in knots. Her teeth chattered, and goose bumps blotted her brown skin. The approaching hovercraft forced her to take cover until it was safe again. *Safe?* she asked herself. No one and nothing was safe from the war machines. Armed to the teeth, they kept colonists at bay and judged, at once, those who'd dare to resist.

Glass broke in a nearby store. A bearded man and two younger boys, covered in filth, dropped food items fleeing the scene.

"Colonists. Stop where you are," ordered an Enforcer. They weren't given a second chance. Curfew violations were punishable by death, and many of the colony's homeless were killed—a systematic cleansing of the undesired.

Now was her chance. She checked both ways and dashed for the other side.

"Halt!" commanded a young soldier.

Two more jumped from the covered deuce and joined their comrade in arms. His name tag read Hawthorne.

"Got us a live one here," congratulated one of the men.

"Now, now. I saw her first. Y'all got to wait ya turn." Hawthorne's speech was slack-jawed, and he spat black tobacco into a cup.

The woman turned her eyes and said, "Please. I mean you no harm. I'm trying to find shelter."

Her words were met with an outburst of laughter. She shunned the red light, and Hawthorne yelled, "Stand straight!"

The scanner finished, and her vision was blurred.

"Fresh off the bus. You know what we do to orange pickers around here, don't ya?"

She watched Hawthorne and his buds move closer. A bit too close for comfort. The ragged coat fell to the side, revealing a tattered shirt and jeans. She shook violently and crossed both her arms and legs.

"You look hungry. How about a little something to chew on?" She turned away from the hand violating her breasts. "Don't be scared. We'll take good care of you."

One of the soldiers stepped away to answer a transmission. The woman was being led by the arm to an alley when the soldier said, "Hey, Tommy. We gotta head to base."

"Can't it wait?" he asked.

"I don't think so. Sup's real pissed."

"Fine." His hands ran down her short brown hair and up again. Hawthorne pulled her once more. This time she was led to the deuce's rear. The flap opened to the faces of frightened immigrants and their children.

Again Hawthorne grabbed her and said, "Not so fast, sweet tush."

"Stop! Stop!" she screamed and kicked.
Whap!

———

Hurry it up! You, over there! Get in line!

The woman came to after hearing the soldier's commands and feeling a thump across her head.

A young girl gripped her mother's hand and stayed close. Her feet were bare, and the doll she held tight was torn from her little arms.

"You won't be needing that where you're going," said Hawthorne.

Outside the deuce, the woman's eyes watered seeing the barbarism before her. Immigrants ushered like cattle down a ramp. Their lives stripped of spirit and dignity. A Hispanic female soldier shied eye contact, clamping an ankle bracelet. After two solid beeps, she moved on. The woman watched the bracelet switch from steady red to green.

"Runner!" alerted a troop. The man's guts exploded from an itchy trigger finger.

"Anyone else?" yelled Hawthorne at the procession. "Didn't think so."

Clank, lock.

The woman was caged along with two other females her age. The beds were scraps of hay twined together. A small hole covered in vileness made for a urinal. They avoided the woman's stares and stayed silent. Hints of dirt remained on newly scrubbed skin.

The reverberation of judgment continued. Whimpers, cries in Spanish went unnoticed. What came next infuriated the woman further.

"Look at it. You can't expect me to pay that kind of money for abused goods," said a male voice. "I don't wanna look at a carved pumpkin sucking my dick. You got anything else?"

"Ah, yes. Come this way," said the dealer. "What do you think?"

"Not bad."

"Young and tender. Nineteen, give or take a year. She'll make a fine housekeeper and play toy. I've tested her myself."

"Too thin. I'll snap the bitch in half."

"I'll throw in her sister for free."

"Too many mouths to feed. What do you take me for, Sergei? A damn fool?"

"No, Mr. Whitman. I only—"

"Shush. Now this one tickles my fancy."

The woman didn't flinch as the two men came into view. The dealer, she presumed, was the short one sporting a skullet. He walked with a slouch and smelled of feces. The suited man walked with prestige, and a briefcase was chained to his wrist. He was clean cut and wore bifocals reminiscent of Benjamin Franklin.

"What's its name?" asked Mr. Whitman.

"Doesn't have one. A port escapee, I'll presume."

The lock twisted, and the cage flung open. "A bit funky. Did you not clean it?"

"She's a new arrival."

"You acknowledge their kind are less than human, yet you speak as though they are. I prefer to see them as decaying matter used for my enjoyment."

"My apologies, sir."

Mr. Whitman fingered the woman's cunt through her jeans. She closed her eyes and took the abuse. "Tight, a bit dry. Nothing I can't fix."

"Would you like to test…it?"

Mr. Whitman looked in the woman's pupils and said, "No need. I'll take it. I don't have much use for these things other than to service my every need. I'll sell it when I've grown weary."

Mr. Whitman blew his fingernails and then held out his wrist. Following a quick transaction, he wiped his wrist on his coat and said, "Scrub it, profile it, and deliver it to my limo."

"Right away, sir."

Into the Darkness

THE LAST TRAIN to arrive was defaced with a bloody hand-print. Below it, written in blood, were the words "keep away." Outside the train, the writer's footprints disappeared into the unknown.

As she leaped to the tracks below, a chilling darkness crept into Raven's bones.

"I'm here."

There's an access door not too far from your location.

"Roger. Out."

The remaining light bulb flickered and then died out. Pitch black changed to green, and Raven kept moving. A cold wind whistled, and not a soul was nearby. Loose advertisements cluttered the tracks. With each step, her conscience repeated "turn back," but she continued. No gangs or runaways hiding from the machines. All was quiet...too quiet.

The train vanished from her peripheral vision. Raven's stomach churned, and she switched to her rifle.

Up and over the platform she went. More blood. Lots of it. A broken lock lay adjacent to the access door. Above it a sign read No Trespassing. Tiffany was on edge but not afraid.

The HUD wavered, and the night vision shorted out.

"I'm running into interference."

The...cl...is...int...the...conn...tion.

She only caught the last part. All communications were cut. She descended into the Cimmerian pit.

The weapon's light revealed a second set of bloody handprints. The Stygian maze and forbidden tunnels haunted her, offering a final warning to return to the surface, where it was safe.

Without Kichiro, she'd have to rely on instinct to navigate this dismal abyss. She came to a T, and against the top of it rested a dead body. His face was peeled and slashed abhorrently. His stomach was torn out, allowing for slimy worms and maggots to feast on what remained. Lifeless eyes were fixed toward the Cimmerian hell from whence his tormentor had emerged.

The light followed bloody three-clawed footprints to where they vanished at the tunnel's corner. Raven's chest quickly rose up and down. Her weapon stayed at eye level, and she watched her footing.

The raw stench of sewage came from ahead. Drips from a shallow ceiling splashed into a red puddle. Another T and more bloodletting. This one had been killed in similar fashion. Two bodies, a trail of blood—they had been running from someone. But who? Or what?

Raven got her answer when an abnormal howl spread throughout the tunnel. The sound was human and wolflike but raspy. She shone the light in every direction, prepared to fire at whatever beast showed itself. She listened to the quick clicking of claws—front, back, left, right. The creature was stalking Raven from its domain.

She glimpsed a grotesque shadow disappearing from the light. Its sharp red eyes brimmed intelligence. A scaly black tail slithered into and out of sight.

All was silent except the slow press of steel on concrete. She listened…waited…stopped.

An unbearable weight forced Raven down, and her weapon flew from her clutches. The rifle toppled beyond her reach. Raven mustered every ounce of strength to fight back; she was inches away from a fanged, salivating snout, a snap away from being eaten alive. In one swift motion, she freed her arm, extracted a blade, and dug it into the beast's neck. Rivers of yellow blood poured from a severed artery. Now flipped over, the beast spasmed for a brief moment and then became still.

She spotted her weapon's light ahead and wasted no time in retrieving it.

The beast was sick and inhuman. Its skin was hard against the barrel. A crossbreed, she reckoned. Half man, half—

A slow, pulsating purple light called her attention away from the creature.

Attached to a wall, midway through Hades, was Carlita's cloaking device. Raven wondered how Carlita had survived long enough to escape. Or had the men who died been used as bait?

Raven, immune to the cloaking device, consulted the Oplink and accessed the deactivation code. A white funnel shorted the diamond-shaped contraption, and its purple light faded. She added a steel fist to finish the job.

Raven.

"Yeah. I'm here."

All systems are go. Good work. It's going to take a minute to get a lock on Carlita.

She traced the funnel over the dead creature's body. "Ever seen anything like this?"

No reply came.

"Kichiro?"

Kichiro's silence was more unsettling than the beast itself. Eventually a reply came. *I'll run an analysis and see what I can find.*

Bittersweet

———◆———

THE WOMAN'S LEGS shook, and she dared not move. Her wet eyes shot to and fro across the luxurious white-walled home. Expensive furs, luminous chandeliers, and lustrous jewels— Mr. Whitman spared no expense decorating his lavish abode.

"Do you speak...ah...En...ga...lish?"

She nodded, and Mr. Whitman snapped, "Good. Come along." He raised one finger to beckon her.

"I'm quite certain you know what will be required of you. Meal preparation, cleaning, servicing me when I see fit—that sort of thing. So I'll spare myself the rhetoric and brainpower of explaining such menial tasks to a beast of burden. But I will add"—she paused on the stairs but then continued to follow him up to the next floor—"every morning you will be washed for my pleasure and wait by my bedside for me to awake from slumber, ready and willing to relieve me."

The two stopped at a bedroom door marked Caution— Live Animal.

"Do not make me have to come looking for you"— Mr. Whitman dipped his glasses and smiled—"Veronica. Ethnic and disgusting. But it'll do."

The door creaked open, and he said, "This is where you will rest, bathe, and shit. There's the bucket and faucet."

Veronica eyed the soap bar on top of a stack of tan tops and bottoms. The bed mattress was hard as a rock, and specks of dried blood covered the one sheet. The malodor of a damp and wooden floor was present.

"A word of warning. My mansion is monitored at all times—even now, in this very room. I hear and see everything. Do not disappoint me, or you will be sorry."

Her arms lifted as the shirt came off.

"Nice and tender, but a bit past your prime, wouldn't you say?" He answered his own question. "Don't speak. It was rhetorical."

Veronica closed and turned her eyes—a bad mistake.

"Don't you ever look away from me!"

Mr. Whitman's squeeze became tighter. Her breast felt as if it would explode.

"On your knees." The belt unzipped. "Make this quick. I have work to do."

She covered her nose at his sweaty-smelling nuts.

"What are you waiting for, you dirty spic? *Chupa mi verga!*"

A whack across the head got her moving. "That's it, my pet. What was your name again? Don't answer just...ugh."

Veronica swallowed Mr. Whitman's musty cock whole.

"Come on. Faster, damn it!" he demanded.

Veronica gagged, and Mr. Whitman said, "Let go. I see you've yet to be properly trained. I'll do it myself."

Obliged to deep throat, Veronica's head became nothing more than a sex toy—a sex toy used and abused for this sick fuck's pleasure. Deeper and deeper he pushed, nearly suffocating her. Out it went, followed by a hard slap to the face, and then it was stuffed back in. Faster and faster. The dick grew harder and harder. Mr. Whitman slowed his pace and then poured hot, unsavory dick juice down Veronica's reddened throat.

Mr. Whitman kicked Veronica onto her hands and knees, yelling, "Swallow it!"

Sweat dripped on the wood. She panted uncontrollably and then guzzled Mr. Whitman's cum. The thick slime made her want to vomit.

"That's a good girl. Don't waste a drop. Right there. Clean it up."

Veronica hesitated, holding her tongue to the wooden floor.

"Clean it!"

He pressed her head and cheek into the floor.

"Lick it, you bitch. Lick it."

Two licks of the tongue, and the floor sparkled with Veronica's saliva.

"How was dinner?" he asked. "You will learn to answer unless I say otherwise. How was dinner?"

"It...wa...was...good."

"Good? So uneducated. I want to hear you say, 'Mr. Whitman, your phallus was toothsome and delightful.'"

"Mr. Whitman, your phallus was..."

"Toothsome."

"Toothsome and delightful."

"Smile. Show your gratitude. Work on both. I want you in tip-top obedience when I rid myself of you."

The door shut, and Mr. Whitman left Veronica violated in her own mess. She touched a loose stitch, and her hand came away from her neck bloody. Fuming, chest and back rising, lips puckered, Veronica vowed revenge.

———

"He was a good man, Governor Batista. He will surely be missed. It's a shame he left us so soon." He gave a small chuckle.

Veronica answered Mr. Whitman's beckoning hand gesture.

"Put a nice shine on it, will you?" he said.

On her knees again. As ordered, she'd fulfilled her morning commitment, fed Mr. Whitman breakfast by hand, and cleaned the dishes.

"No, stupid. Shine my fucking shoes." Rolling his eyes, he continued the previous conversation.

Veronica retrieved a shoe-shine kit from her shirt pouch and kept an ear open.

Talk of Sadiq's death had spread like wildfire. Mr. Whitman pretended to care and spoke of funeral arrangements. Nothing about Mr. Whitman was remotely compassionate. He was the embodiment of arrogance and self-entitlement. Advanced degrees, certifications, and a love-me wall decorated the marble-floored office.

"Have they located the woman from the museum?" he asked the governor, sipping a whiskey. "Interesting."

Veronica could only speculate about the governor's words, due to Mr. Whitman's surgically implanted earpiece. His voice deepened, his responses were brief yes and no answers, and she felt eyes staring down at her.

"No change comes without bloodshed. Their blood. A new era is upon us. A new era of man and…machine."

The blood of the innocent spilled to usher in a worldwide dystopia. Veronica quickly polished a dropped tear, making it unnoticeable.

"Well, I believe they'll come around. They always do. It's most unfortunate it happened this way."

She finished the second shoe and sat upright, humiliated into behaving like a human dog.

"President Batista. I like the sound of that."

President? she thought. The last president had been nearly two centuries ago. The new constitution guaranteed each colony's independence, except in times of war. This could only mean one thing: there was no constitution.

"Good day, Mr. President."

Veronica stood and waited for additional commands.

"All done? Don't answer." Mr. Whitman massaged his baby-skinned chin, admiring his reflection in the polished shoes. "Not bad. Handsome, aren't I? *Aren't I?*"

"Mr. Whitman, you are exquisitely handsome on this exuberant morning."

"Impressive. You've been studying your dictionary. Good girl. Here, have a treat; say 'ah.'"

"Ah." The first ripened piece of banana hit Veronica's nose.

"Oh my, I seem to have missed. I was never any good at basketball. Stay open." He tried again. "Hole in one!"

Veronica swallowed the moist fruit. It was the only bite she'd had since slurping Mr. Whitman's cum off the bedroom floor.

"More?" he asked.

Her conscience argued. *But I'm so hungry.* "Please, Mr. Whitman. Feed me more doggy treats."

"I would love to stay and play, but I have work to do."

Mr. Whitman locked the briefcase to his wrist and saw Veronica out of his office. Two solid beeps and then a red bar appeared on the door's pad.

"This evening, you will prepare a meal for me and my guest. I will not tell you what to prepare. Put that peanut-sized brain of yours to good use. But no Mexican, chink food, or fried chicken. Just uttering those words repulses me."

A silver-suited man opened the limo, and Mr. Whitman said, "Oh, and Veronica? Remember: I hear and see everything."

Any further outside and she'd lose an ankle. Death was her only escape.

Ghost

Emerald Colony, Southern Port, December 15, 2172

Two SECURITY GUARDS and one armored deuce were unloading passengers. Raven adjusted the range finder and watched a hovercraft touch down.

"Well, I'll be damned."

What you see?

"He couldn't resist, could he?"

Bishop Emmanuel studied his surroundings before being led into the facility.

"You don't find it a bit odd that she'd make it so easy?"

The beacon is lagging. That's the last known location I was able to get a fix on. While you dozed off last night, I found a few things that might interest you.

"That train car was a five-star hotel in my book. Enlighten me."

It appears a couple of curious scientists got their hands dirty playing DNA games. It's a perfect facial match for a human, but I'm going to need a sample of the creature's blood.

"I'll let you scrape it off me when I get back."

An early-morning snowstorm allowed for closer reconnaissance. A single A51 patrolled the airspace around the massive wall, only to disappear beyond it. Reinforced concrete, unmanned weaponized watchtowers—something didn't sit right. The port hadn't been nearly so heavily guarded when she'd tried to escape years ago. As a teen, she remembered nearly making it, until a snaggletoothed, beer-bellied guard snatched her up. Avoiding detection seemed more impossible now than ever. One observation boggled her mind: the weapons weren't pointed inward; they faced out.

"Coast is clear," she transmitted. "I'm up." She used the Oplink to transform her armor's colors to match the snowy terrain.

Roger that. Once you take Carlita into custody, I'll have a transport en route.

"Copy."

She silenced her weapon. Raven's boots became caked in snow as she came down the hill. An old guard shack was her next way point.

Raven moved undetected across the access road to cover. She monitored the weapons, but they didn't bulge.

Another quick dash brought her within range.

Her armor slightly vibrated from the deuce's engine. She hacked the driver's communications system and listened to the dialogue of two soldiers.

"I'm not going back out there. Has he seen the fucking weather lately?"

"The superintendent's not happy with your crew. He says that on the way home, he saw slews of unregistered on the street."

"We just brought over a shit ton."

"You know how he is. Make another round, and you guys can cut loose."

"This is stupid."

"Don't shoot the messenger."

"Fuck you, Floyd."

"Bite me, Hawthorne."

A wad of dip hit the snow, followed by two boots. The deuce's door slammed, and she listened to Hawthorne urinate just feet away. The stream of piss stopped, and he started to investigate the footprints.

She said under her breath, "Don't do it, kid."

Lazy or just plain uninterested, Hawthorne abandoned investigating the footprints and returned to the deuce.

"Let's go," said a soldier, returning to the vehicle.

"You won't believe this," said an infuriated Hawthorne. "We gotta go back out."

"What?"

"Yup. Dumb ass at control said so."

"Hey. Who did that?"

Raven knew he was referring to her trail of footprints.

"I don't know, man."

"This place creeps me out, being close to the wall and all. You ever been outside?"

"Don't be stupid. Of course not. No one goes outside the wall. You and I both know that."

"Yeah, man. Well, I heard the people out there turned into freaks."

"Your mom's a freak."

"No, I'm serious, man. My uncle told me they started transforming, like werewolves or some shit."

"For real?"

"Yeah, man. My uncle used to be night conductor. He told me one night, on one of his last runs, he hit something that jumped out in front. He said since no people were in the cars, he stopped and got out to take a look."

"Oh yeah? What he see?"

"It wasn't there no more. Like, it just vanished. My uncle's never been the same since."

"Whatever, man."

"Talk to him. He'll tell you the same thing."

Raven analyzed the soldier's voice and profile. It would prove useful later. She timed her movements with the deuce and crept through the gate undetected. Taking up cover behind a fuel tank, she saw that the remaining enemy locater was attached to a satellite dish. The same two guards had departed the area of responsibility, and several human subjects lay curled in cages. Two men could be seen walking together up and down the aisle.

She'd never let them catch her. Something's off, thought Raven. She gripped both ends of a rusty ladder and began to climb, but suddenly she froze in place.

Spotting the A51's searchlight in time was the only reason she stayed alive. Its glowing tail disappeared once more out of sight.

Raven watched Bishop Emmanuel select a young girl. A woman cried out, only to be slapped down.

"Enough of this shit."

Shards of broken glass toppled down from the ceiling. The cowardly bishop fled from the fallen dark angel. But he wasn't fast enough. The little girl ran to her mother's cage, and Bishop Emmanuel's neck was placed in a choke hold.

Pop! Sergei grabbed his ankle and fell down.

Raven didn't afford the bishop the dignity of a painless death.

"Enrico says, 'Fuck off.'" She switched her rifle to burst mode, and three silenced rounds spilled his brains.

Pew! Pew! The guards dropped like flies.

A heavy boot smashed Sergei's fractured ankle into the floor.

"Ahh!"

"Where's Carlita?"

"I don't know who you're talking about!" cried Sergei.

Slice. Off went his fingers with a blade.

"My fingers!"

"We'll try this again, you fat, disgusting fuck."

"I don't—" A jab to the pelvic region split his balls open. He screamed in agony, flailing on the ground. Sergei held his pelvis and coughed up blood as he spoke. "There was a woman here last night. I...I...I sold her off."

"To whom?"

"To Mr. Whitman...please!" he begged.

"Did you get that?"

Every last bit of it, transmitted Kichiro. The picture of a snarky-faced bastard came into view.

That's him, all right. WAR's second-in-command. If Carlita infiltrated—Raven, you have incoming.

"I need a drop."

Now is not a good time.

"Not for me. I'm getting these captives out of here."

There won't be enough time. You need to go.

"I'll make time."

Damn it. Sending one now.

Raven inserted the gauntlet's blade into Sergei's rectum. "Ahh! Ahh! Ahh!" His spine came next.

The armor's EMP capabilities shorted the locks, freeing the captives. Two males armed themselves with the guards' rifles and prepared to defend the immigrants.

Raven, your initial way point will be the XP. Go now!

She spotted the deuce trucking along the deep, snowy embankment. One man held the front and the other the rear.

"To the hillside. Move!" Raven protected the flank as fifteen captives sloshed through the heavy snow.

"Momma! Momma!" screamed the little girl. She stood by her mother, who'd become too weak to run. A young man and Raven ran to the back of the line. He picked up the injured woman and carried her.

A bright light landed on the hill, and the A51 became visible.

Thump, thump...BOOM!

A big ball of flame fell from the storm and landed fifty meters from the deuce.

Small-arms fire struck the man carrying the woman. A streak of blood ran from his stomach down. He didn't let go. Hawthorne and his crew took up defensive fighting positions and were firing at anyone who moved.

Child pressed against her armor, Raven lit up Hawthorne and his men. They were no more.

Raven, JTF fighters are en route. Get those passengers onboard.

The armed men protected the immigrants as they loaded into the transport.

They're closing in.

"That's the last of them! Get 'em out here!"

Raven made a break for it. A blue light held the transport's undercarriage as it rose. A fired missile chased the transport, and she witnessed the hyperspace system zip the transport to the heavens just in time.

Sacrifice

VERONICA FINISHED SERVING Mr. Whitman and his guest a juicy roast-beef dinner with all the fixings—mashed potatoes, green beans, and sauerkraut. She had to force herself to keep down the slice of expired ham and bread she'd eaten. Veronica never knew if or when she would eat again.

She refilled wine glasses and served cheesecake for dessert. Her stomach growled at the strawberry topping, and she imagined devouring every piece of it.

A tall, handsome, and well-dressed Hispanic man sat with his legs crossed and fingers laced. By the looks of him, Veronica assumed he'd never suffered at the merciless hands of Sadiq or his enterprise.

"Mr. President," said Mr. Whitman. He chuckled.

"We've been business partners for decades, Theo. Stop with the formalities."

"The stage has been set for the ceremony."

"That was rather quick. I take it England signed the constitution?"

"The strong arm of persuasion helped them fall in line."

England? What did this all mean? Veronica benefited from Mr. Whitman's assumption that she had a monkey's brain. He talked rather freely about politics and technology of a sensitive nature. But no matter where he went, the briefcase never left his side, except at night when he locked it in his office.

"I was correct in believing the simpleminded of the lot would resist. So I've arranged a live broadcast at Fort Emery's headquarters."

"To a new era."

"A new era of man."

The two toasted. Raul Batista looked at Veronica but directed his words at Mr. Whitman. "A fine specimen. How much did this one cost?"

"Not as much as Sergei tried to swindle from my pockets. Have at it, if you will."

"While I appreciate your generosity, I'll pass," replied Raul.

"Perhaps another time."

Raul stood up and said, "I'm afraid I must be going."

"Well, it has been a pleasure having you as my guest of honor this evening, Raul."

Veronica noticed Mr. Whitman had trouble standing from his cushy leather sofa and used its arm for balance. She listened to Mr. Whitman lock the door behind Raul.

"Oh, Veronica!" the drunken buffoon called out to her. Mr. Whitman stumbled in her direction.

Slap! "Answer me when I call you, you stupid bitch," he said in a sloshed manner.

Slap! "Fucking Mexican whore. Look at you. Pathetic."

Slap!

Veronica's eyes teared up, and her lips quivered. Off his belt came. The pants dropped, and shirt buttons popped.

"Undress, and get on your knees."

She obeyed, and the belt lashed her bare skin. Lash upon brutish lash tore at her flesh, and Mr. Whitman laughed at her cries. He finished a nearby bottle of wine and threw it at the fireplace. A burst of flame jetted out, and then the fire settled.

"Now...on your back."

The wounds on Veronica's shoulder seeped blood.

Whap! Whap! Whap! Whap!

She saw the belt plop on the carpet and listened to the sizzle of coals being prodded. Branded like a piece of meat, Veronica screamed out. Mr. Whitman scalded her back with the poker stick, mocking his tortured victim, all the while jerking his cock as he spread his legs over her body. She felt splats of jizz sting her open wounds.

"Clean this mess you've made," said Mr. Whitman. "Sunny side up, fresh squeezed, hold the bacon."

He retrieved the briefcase and, again, left Veronica festering in filth.

———

Blood swirled down the drain from a squished rag. Veronica dipped it in the brown water again and placed the cold rag on her wounds. How much more could she take? The beatings and abuse were becoming too much to bear. It had taken three hours to clean the dining area and living room, stopping every so often to care for a wound. In five hours, she'd be required to prepare breakfast and wait by Mr. Whitman's bedside. The opportunity to slit Mr. Whitman's throat presented itself, but that would be too easy. His time would come.

Veronica eyed the black camera broadcasting her misery to the world. She took a seat on the hard bed and closed her eyes, waiting and listening. Finally she was given the signal.

The lights blacked out, the camera powered off, and she heard the deep roar of the Lunar Crystal generator as it shut down. She pushed open the door to her slave quarters and headed for Mr. Whitman's unsecured office. She lifted the briefcase and a pistol from the desk and aimed for his bedroom.

Wham!

The door flew open, and Veronica yanked the covers from Mr. Whitman. Naked and dazzled, he stared wide eyed at the escaped slave.

"Veronica! What are you doing?"

Time was running out.

Veronica led Mr. Whitman into the living room at gunpoint. The mansion's fireplace flickered in the darkness.

She shot both kneecaps, forcing him to kneel.

"Please—anything you want," he begged. "I'll let you go."

"Say 'ah,' motherfucker." She rammed the hot poker into Mr. Whitman's mouth and watched him scream. She grabbed his hair and held his face in the fire. The smell of burning flesh was pleasing to the nose. With his face as black as charcoal, he squirmed and rolled on the floor.

Her head was down, her chest heaving, her hair wet and matted, and the light from the fire reflected off Veronica's sweaty body and bleeding wounds. She felt the hunter's presence. She looked up, without turning around, and said, "She knew you'd come."

"It's over."

A weapon charged, but Veronica couldn't care less.

Veronica faced Raven and said, "You're a fool. You do their bidding, confused about what side to take."

"Drop it!" ordered Raven.

Veronica put a bullet into Mr. Whitman's skull and discarded the pistol.

Veronica stopped herself from opening the briefcase. She said, "My people have suffered long enough."

"You go through with this, and we all will suffer," said Raven.

Veronica's head snapped back from Carlita's bullet. Blood streamed from a steaming hole, and her eyes rolled up in her head. A cold but necessary sacrifice.

"Drop your weapon," said Carlita. "You're good. But you are no hunter." She stripped Raven of her weapon and side arm. Piece by piece, she dismantled them, rendering the weapons unserviceable. "First rule of hunting: everyone's your enemy."

Raven's knee caved in, from Carlita's kick, and she dropped. Carlita clocked her cold with the butt of the gun, and she fell face first.

The final piece of the puzzle had fallen into place. With the computer and location of WAR's central AI system, Carlita had the power to shut down the planet.

She saw a red blip flashing on Mr. Whitman's wrist and listened to the approaching machines. A quick shot from her laser into the fireplace, and flames rapidly spread inside the mansion.

Outside, in the snowy pastures, she watched the shuttle descend from a snow-misted sky while silhouetted against a full moon.

Did she think I would come so easily?

Aborted

"You sent me on a fucking suicide mission," said Raven, coming down the ramp.

"We had no idea Carlita was capable of removing the barcode. It was clearly unconceivable," said Will, trying to keep up.

Raven tossed a sweaty towel into a trash can and exited the bay. She recognized the two Latino males who had helped in the escape. Their faces were filled with admiration, respect, and gratitude. She returned a nod their way.

"I need you in the field."

Raven stopped. "Why?"

"Right now, you're the best I've got. No one else would have saved those captives," whispered Will. "That took tremendous courage. You're made for this."

"Spare me the shit, Will."

"Carlita's headed for Chicago. It's where WAR's central AI system is located. You'll be well equipped for the entire mission."

Chicago? It made sense for WAR to build their system in the abandoned city. No one would dare think of infiltrating the facility deep underground. If she entertained the idea of returning to Earth, she knew drops would be out the question.

"How close can you get me?" she asked as they entered her quarters.

"You'll go in by parachute, near the city's center. The system's underneath the city, and she's going to run into trouble trying to access it."

"Tiffany!" yelled a bright-eyed Enrico.

Soon Raven found little arms grasped around her aching waist. She endured the pain and kissed her son on the head. It felt so good to see her little one again. When she opened her eyes, a cold feeling ran down her chest. She stopped breathing and felt weak in the knees.

The woman and girl she'd rescued stood at the door. She had a gut feeling about exactly who she was looking at. Enrico ran back to the woman and child. The woman embraced Enrico and said, "*Gracias, senorita*, for bringing us together again."

———

She felt the rush of steam penetrating her pores. Water pelted off her sore body. Her eyes turned toward the drain, watching specks of dirt and tears spiral away. She wanted so badly to turn off her emotions, to feel nothing. But love wouldn't allow such an easy exit. In hindsight, she cursed herself for not snatching Enrico from the woman's arms. But she had no right. Enrico wasn't her son. He belonged to someone else. She'd learned that the young man who'd died was Enrico's older brother.

The pain was too much bear.

Clip, clip. Strands of black hair fell on the bathroom's floor. Her hair now cut to ear length, Raven flapped her bangs over one eye and stared at her own reflection. Anger, rage, and hate merged as one. The mirror spider-webbed.

———

"Hey! You can't be in here," said a maintenance worker. His hands went up, and he stepped back.

Up the ladder, Raven threw her rucksack and rifle into the VTOL's navigator seat. She lowered the window on the cockpit and fired up the engine. She'd taken a crash course in operating the craft by studying the Oplink's files.

Raven, what do you think you're doing? transmitted Will. His face appeared in the VTOL's HUD. She cut the feed.

Workers cleared the area, running to safety. At full speed, Raven zipped into outer space.

Among the Ruins

Chicago, Illinois, December 16, 2172

WITH ONE LAST push, the hatch came off its hinges. The hard landing had destroyed most of the shuttle, and Carlita had almost given up hope of ever escaping. Her breath clouded into the cold and dark night. Ice bit her toes and her gloved fingers. She charged her carbine and leaped from the shuttle into the ruins of a city long since forgotten. Or was it?

From supposedly abandoned windows, she felt eyes watching her every move. Scavengers, hunters, cannibals—whatever lurked within those walls had evolved and adapted to its environment in nearly two centuries in darkness.

Her target lay miles ahead. This was the final stretch to freedom. She'd have to remain as alert as ever to survive.

She'd been traveling a little more than ten minutes when an unexpected noise caught her off guard. A trash can, blown over by a strong gust of icy wind, rolled to a stop. Carlita's heart was beating so hard that it felt as if it might rip a hole in her chest, and she lowered the rifle. So frostbitten. So grim. How did any of them survive?

She pulled the skullcap over her ears and continued on. She avoided the sidewalks to keep her distance; the alleys were just as dangerous. She came across a tiny black rock sparkling with green ooze. Ground zero. She expected to see more of the same.

A chilling howl filled the night air. Carlita scanned the rooftops and abandoned windows for the creature. It was close. She could feel it, could almost smell its disgusting sewer-like stench. Another howl gripped her bones but from a different direction. Then a third. The beasts were in communication, signaling to one another, formulating a carnivorous plan to slay their prey. The quick clicks of their claws sounded unseen between ominous buildings. Their raspy cries scratched at her nerves. From the shadows, one appeared and then ducked out of sight again. She saw murderous red eyes and sharp yellow fangs salivating for warm, succulent flesh.

Carlita shot two rounds into a window but missed her target. Screeching howls, brewing with infuriation, pierced her ears. A slight tapping of claws came from behind her but then stopped.

There, in the black and frigid night, stood a demon summoned from the bowels of hell. Hot breath rose from its wet nostrils. It paced on its hind legs before dropping to all fours.

The beast charged Carlita, but she took it down with one shot to its thick head. A window shattered, and then she laid to rest another beast as it lunged at her. But she was slow to react and found herself fighting a third. A rifle smack to the face only pissed it off. Escaping its large arms, she rolled under it, extracted her pistol, and shot it dead center in its blackened heart. The grotesque pile of meat plopped on the road, bleeding yellow ooze from its dying body. That was the last of them—for now. There'd be more if she didn't hurry.

———

Raven kept her head down and waited for a break in fire. Two soldiers' heads split open from the rain of her RK72. The rising sun glared off an approaching Goliath. Its glass blew apart from a launched grenade, and the operator became a bloody liquid. A sniper fired from the crumbling Sears Tower. Raven returned the favor and watched the sniper fall to his death.

WAR had used their technology to create an electrical conducive perimeter around the tower. It was weak but allowed for the resupply of weapons and equipment. They'd been stupid enough to turn the lights on, revealing their position from miles away. The remains of creatures and humans were scattered everywhere. She'd recognized the skeleton of an infant cradled in its mother's arms.

Additional small-arms fire could be heard not too far from her location. A whistle caught her attention, and she jumped for cover.

Boom!

Pop-pop...pop-pop!

Raven switched magazines and fired upon soldiers as she dashed across the street. They were no match for her. She would never have believed she'd be killing men in uniform, but they'd left her few options. The force was thin, possibly because WAR had never expected to come under attack by those outside the wall. Their only concern was with what lay beneath.

Raven witnessed Carlita make a break for an unmanned VTOL. Her body sore as hell, Raven gave it all she had. She knew exactly what Carlita was planning to do.

In one massive leap, Raven grabbed the wing of the VTOL and held on. She didn't look down as the craft ascended to the top of the tower.

The firing of a weapons system stung her eardrums. Armored soldiers were being shredded alive. Raven dropped from the craft onto the roof, and her rucksack broke her fall.

The madwoman slid back the cockpit's window and jumped down. Carlita kicked the hunter's weapon out of her hand. A boot to the face bloodied Raven's nose. Carlita pulled the briefcase from her rucksack and said, "Witness as an empire burns."

Carlita had never intended to infiltrate WAR. She knew she would never make it. Instead, she planned to become a martyr.

Raven pulled her strength together and tackled Carlita. The briefcase slid to the edge of the tower. Raven got one punch in before Carlita flipped her over. On her feet again, Raven gave Carlita a roundhouse kick in the head. Carlita blocked the follow-up and delivered furious blows to Raven's stomach. Raven held her stomach, and Carlita's leg came down on her neck.

Wham!

"You dumb bitch," said Carlita, retrieving the computer. "You think I was stupid enough to believe Sadiq would give me the AI's code?"

Carlita was planning to use WAR's armed satellites against them. She brought the satellites online, raised her arms, and closed her eyes.

"Carlita, no!" screamed Raven.

Beep.

Carlita's chest exploded from Raven's bullet, and she fell sideways.

Raven looked to the cold blue sky and saw two glimmers of light. Holding her bruised stomach and panting, she limped to the VTOL. Raven climbed in and typed in the *Virginia*'s coordinates. The craft took off vertically, and Raven blasted away before she could be roasted alive.

Two blue beams hit the tower's antennae, and the Sears Tower exploded in sections from the top down. A wave of fire spread across what was left of downtown Chicago, leveling everything in its path.

Distant Memories

Milky Way Galaxy, January 1, 2173

ENRICO KISSED HIS mom and said, "I wanna sleep next to Tiffany."

Gabrielle happily agreed and said to Raven, "I can't thank you enough for all you've done. Just so you know, he asked to keep the name."

"It's no big deal. Get some rest."

A medic helped Enrico adjust in his soft pod. Then the lid closed, and Enrico drifted off to sleep. His sister, Sharon, opted to sleep next to Chelsea.

Most of the second level was already under cryogenic sleep. Will came down from the first level to join Raven.

"You sure you wanna do this?" he asked.

"So where we headed?" she asked in return, without answering his question.

"I think you mean, where are *you* headed?"

Raven's eyebrows raised.

"I received a message from command concerning the distress signal."

"Who sent it?"

"Logan."

Raven couldn't believe her ears. "Logan departed Earth over a hundred years ago."

"March 1994, to be exact."

"Months before the comet hit."

Will kept his voice low and said, "I'm not liking the way things are looking. Logan discovered a way to travel between dimensions, and something tells me that when we find him, he won't be alone."

"Do you think they'll survive?" she asked, looking out into space.

"Only time will tell. Our work is done. Earth's future is now in their hands."

Raven lay down and took a deep breath. The pod slowly closed, and finally she felt at peace.

To be continued…